Here are some very unsettling stories, all designed to send shivers up your spine. There's Billy the bully, who develops a mysterious mark on his thumb while on a school outing to the Castle; a monster in a washing machine – out for revenge; a girl whose mind is taken over by a camera; and the class that has a ghost as one of its members . . .

"Adèle Geras aims not so much at the quick surprise as at the effect of quietly mounting tension."   *Observer*

Adèle Geras

Letters of Fire

and other unsettling stories

Lions

For Angela, Ralph and Carey Young

First published in Great Britain 1984
by Hamish Hamilton Children's Books
First published in Lions 1986
Second impression November 1989

Lions is an imprint of
the Children's Division, part of
the Collins Publishing Group,
8 Grafton Street, London W1X 3LA

"Billy's Hand" first appeared in
The Methuen Book of Strange Tales, published 1980
"The Doll Maker" first appeared in
The Methuen Book of Sinister Stories, published 1982

Printed and bound in Great Britain by
William Collins Sons & Co. Ltd, Glasgow

Contents

1 Letters of Fire   1
2 Live Music   26
3 Billy's Hand   37
4 The Poppycrunch Kid   52
5 Mirror   71
6 The Doll Maker   93
7 The Graveyard Girl   105
8 The Light of Memory   134

1 Letters of Fire

Between the fishmonger's and the lampshade shop on Sidney Street, you'll find the Kwik and Spik launderette. Most people walk past without even seeing it. The yellow paint is peeling from around the grimy window. On the floor, linoleum tiles which started life as black and white have aged to grey and grey, and the squat, blue machines, four to each wall, glare at one another across a double row of orange plastic chairs. The Kwik and Spik doesn't exactly have to turn customers away. Since the opening of the Speedy Washeteria round the corner (coffee machine, fabric softener dispenser, padded seats and next door to the chip shop into the bargain) it's mainly the Regulars who still frequent it. These are: Miss Clutterbuck, who wears a tartan headscarf and slippers at all times, Mr. Steel, who has very few clothes to wash, but comes in for the company, Mr. Rafferty, who fills his machine with denim boiler suits and overalls although it's common knowledge that he hasn't worked for years, and Mrs. Harding, who has seen better days. As her laundry goes round and round, she tells the other Regulars (round and round like the machines she goes: they've heard the story over and over) how once upon a time all her delicate blouses were washed and ironed by hand, each tuck individually pressed, every petticoat white and frothy as a bridal veil, and all her husband's shirts starched into such a shiny stiffness that they barely needed him to fill them out at all. The others listen, and nod and feed yoghurt cartons of Blaze 100 with Miracle GX22 to sad little bundles of nylon socks and Courtelle cardigans and tea towels on which the stains never seem to fade although the colours have long ago disappeared. Sometimes students come in. They have a frivolous attitude to their laundry. Bung it in and go off round the corner to the pub till it's done. Quite often, seeing the cycle is finished, Mr. Steel will kindly open the machine and put the wet clothes into a basket.

"I took your clothes out for you," he says when the student returns from her carousing. There is a hint of reproach in his voice.

"Oh, ta!" says the student, only half-listening, then shoves the twisted garments into the drier any old how, and vanishes once more.

There is a dingy two-room flat above the Kwik and Spik. Mavis Moon and her son George have lived there for five years. Mavis works long hours at the Dairy down the road. She is a thin, nervous woman. She looks old before her time. No wonder, say the Regulars, no husband and that little boy to look after all on her own. The

2

boy is known as Moony, not only because of his name, but because he moons about in the launderette between the end of school and his bedtime, most of Saturday and for the greater part of the holidays.

"It's not right," says Mrs. Harding. "A child should have other children to play with."

"Nowhere for kids to play, though, is there?" says Mr. Rafferty.

"We wouldn't want them tearing round in here, now, would we?"

"He could take a friend upstairs to play," suggests Miss Clutterbuck. "Or watch television or something."

"There isn't room to swing a cat up there," says Mr. Steel. "I've been. I came over all funny one day and Mrs. Moon kindly took me up. And gave me a cup of tea, as well. They haven't got much furniture up there, you know, and it's a blessing really, 'cos if they did have, there wouldn't be anywhere to put it."

"Still," says Mrs. Harding, "he's a very strange child. Doesn't talk much, does he? Always looks half asleep to me. It can't be right, can it? Sometimes I feel sorry for him. He seems . . ." she lowers her voice and almost mouths the next words, "not quite right in the head."

The Regulars tut and cough and turn their eyes back to their own clothes, foaming away behind glass. The Kwik and Spik is silent, save for the ocean rumblings of the machines and the occasional rhythmic tapping of a buckle or a button on the metal drums.

A few months ago, the Kwik and Spik was vandalized. Nothing too dreadful: a few slogans, the odd heart and arrow done in felt tip.

"Bound to happen," said Miss Clutterbuck knowingly. "It's those students."

Nothing really serious, you'd have thought, but the owners of the Kwik and Spik thought otherwise and that is why they sent a Guardian Angel down to watch over their property, a person called Hilda Bolt. The most dastardly vandal, the heaviest of heavy rockers, the punkest of punks, the coolest of all the cool word-scribblers would blench and run when confronted by her, oh yes. It was impossible to picture Hilda Bolt in her pram or as a young child. She looked as though she had been carefully designed in some workshop, specifically in order to repel vandals, ne'er do wells, layabouts and ninety nine per-cent of the population besides. A yellow nylon overall covered arms which would have been a credit to Popeye after a can of spinach. Her eyes, pale blue and white, like marbles, looked out over the hills and valleys of her beige, wrinkled cheeks. The workshop designer had not wasted time on a mouth. An opening in her face in which to balance a cigarette, a slit to mutter threats through – what else should a mouth be for? Smiling? No one at the Kwik and Spik had ever seen her teeth. Kissing? Easier to imagine a rhinoceros doing such a thing. After the initial shock, the Regulars hardly noticed her. You had to say this for her, she was not given to idle chatter. She had her own chair, up in the corner by the driers, and there she sat, night and day, smoking or muttering or turning the greasy pages of a magazine. Occasionally, she darted baleful looks at the machines, or the students or even the Regulars.

She reserved her real hatred for Moony, the boy from the flat upstairs. Everyone noticed it. She was rough with him. Unnecessarily cruel.

"They're oil and water," Miss Clutterbuck said. "They just don't mix, that's all. Some folk are like that, you know. Can't stand kiddies. Not at any price."

"It's having none of her own," said Mr. Steel. "She doesn't know how to handle him."

"We don't know if she's got kids or not, do we?" Mr. Rafferty put in. "Never says nowt. Never even said if she's a Missis or a Miss."

The idea that there might be a Mr. Bolt somewhere, even some little Bolts, stunned the Regulars into silence for a long moment. At last Mrs. Harding said: "The child's terrified of her. You can see that. I think it's a shame."

"What I can't understand," said Mr. Rafferty, "is why he comes in here all the time, then. He doesn't have to, does he? He could stay up there in the flat and never lay eyes on our Hilda."

"He'd be all alone, though, wouldn't he?" Mrs. Harding said. "With his mum working till gone seven, most nights. Anyway, I think," she blushed, "well, I know it sounds silly but that's kids all over isn't it? I think those machines are like toys to him. He speaks to them. I've watched him. They're like his friends . . ." she broke off quickly as Moony made his way into the launderette.

"Hello, Moony," said Miss Clutterbuck. "Had a good day at school?"

"Yes. Thanks." said Moony, looking towards the corner where Hilda Bolt was sitting in the manner of one checking to see that a fierce dog is safely chained up. She looked up from her magazine and looked away again. Moony shivered and crouched down beside one of the machines.

Mrs. Harding whispered to Miss Clutterbuck:

"There. Did you see that? Did you see the look she gave him? You can cut the atmosphere with a knife when they're both in here together."

"He seems all right now," Miss Clutterbuck whispered back.

"In a world of his own, he looks. Often wonder what he's thinking about."

Moony thought: She's like a spider. That's what she reminds me of, sitting there. In the corner. I wish a giant foot would come out of the sky and squash her flat. I hate her. Can you hear in there? Are you listening? She's horrible. I'll tell you something. Are you there? I know you are. I can hear you. Slurp swish click. I can see you in the soap bubbles. Behind the clothes, peeping out. So listen to me. She hurts me. See this bruise? That's her. She kicks me when no one's looking. Once, she pushed me and I banged my head on a chair. All these bruises on my legs, that's her. And my arms. She pinches me. Tugs my hair when no one's here. Says I shouldn't be in here. Shouldn't be allowed. Why not? I asked her, why not? She said it worried the customers. But it doesn't. They're nice to me. They talk to me sometimes, but I can't think what to say, so I shut up, most of the time. I expect they think I'm daft. At school that's what they think. They call it slow there. I'm a little slow. There aren't many customers in here anyway. Are you still there? Can you hear me? Show me that you're there. Please. Please do something. Show me.

"Miss Bolt!" Mr. Steel said, "could you just give us a hand with this door, please? It seems to be stuck."

Hilda Bolt looked up from her magazine.

"Give it a kick," she said, not moving.

"I don't rightly like to," said Mr. Steel, "I might scratch the paint or something. I wouldn't like to be responsible." Hilda Bolt shook her head, sighed and rose heavily to her feet.

"You," she said to Moony who was kneeling beside the machine, "shift yourself." Her thick fingers took hold of his jacket by the collar and half-lifted, half-pushed him on to one of the chairs.

"Let me look," she grunted, and peered into the glass. She fiddled with the lock. Nothing. She kicked the front of the machine over and over again. Nothing.

"Oh dear," said Mrs. Harding. "Whatever shall we do? Poor Mr. Steel. All his clothes are in there."

The Regulars and Hilda Bolt went into a huddle round the door. Police, Fire Department, leave it till tomorrow and call the engineers. The voices, the suggestions rose and fell . . . waves of sound. No one noticed Moony, whispering into the small opening at the top of the machine. Quickly, quietly whispering.

"I'll call the engineers tomorrow, Mr. Steel. That's the best I can do," said Hilda Bolt, making her way back to the corner. "There's nothing can happen to your clothes in there, you know."

As she passed, she thumped the top of the machine with her fist, and the glass door flew open.

"Oh, my word," said Mr. Steel, delighted. "That did the trick. Well done, and thank you." He beamed at Hilda Bolt, who shrugged and settled herself into her chair.

Mr. Steel began to remove his wet clothes. He always took them out one by one and shook them carefully, and laid them neatly in the basket, almost folding them before putting them into the drier. A shirt came out first this time. Mr. Steel held it up and his mouth fell open. Moony was watching from his chair. Mr. Steel opened and closed his mouth several times. He seemed to be gasping for air. At last:

"Look at this!" he squeaked. "Mrs. Harding! Miss Clutterbuck! Mr. Rafferty! Look what's happened to my shirt." He was trembling all over.

"Oh, heavens, how dreadful, Mr. Steel," said Mrs. Harding, and her hand flew to her mouth. "It's ruined. Completely ruined."

"How did it happen?" This was Mr. Rafferty.

"I can't think. I didn't have anything with hooks or buckles in there. How?"

"It looks," said Miss Clutterbuck, "as if it's been gone over with a rake. Look at it. It's in shreds. I mean, you'd only know it was a shirt from the collar."

"Maybe you can claim compensation," suggested Mr. Rafferty.

"I'd better get the rest of my things out," said Mr. Steel. "It's my best shirt . . . it was."

"One of those students," said Miss Clutterbuck, "most probably left a brooch or something in there."

Moony watched in silence as Mr. Steel took out his clothes. Every single one of them was ruined. Mr. Steel was almost in tears, so Mr. Rafferty took him out to the pub for a brandy to help him over the shock. Mrs. Harding and Miss Clutterbuck put their heads together and began to draft a letter to the owners of the Kwik and Spik launderette.

Hilda Bolt muttered as she taped a notice saying 'Out of Order' on to the machine which had caused all the trouble. Moony looked into Mr. Steel's basket. Some of the clothes were torn, shredded, as if by huge claws rending the fabric over and over again. Others were unrecognizable: the smaller garments had been reduced almost to pulp. They seemed to have been chewed up. Moony glanced at Hilda Bolt in her corner. She was busy filling in the crossword, busy in her fat spider world, not looking at him at all. He crept towards the machine, looked inside at the holes in the metal drum, put his hand in to feel if there were any loose bits of metal that could have damaged the clothes, but the drum was cool and smooth: silver and smooth and cool. Nothing. Moony patted the top of the machine. He put his lips close to the square opening where the soap went in and whispered:

"Now I know you're there."

"What are you doing with that machine, you dozy little beggar?" came Hilda Bolt's voice, so hard it hurt Moony's ears.

"Nothing." (You spider. Fat ugly spider. Squashed spider.)

"Then get away from it, you hear? This minute."

She came lumbering across the floor towards him, one arm above her head. He fled for the door, but not before she had caught him. By the hair.

"Ow," he moaned. "That hurts. Leave me alone."

"Get out of here and up them stairs where you belong, and don't let me see you in here again tonight. We've got enough bloody problems without you. Now shift yourself."

"I'm allowed in here," Moony was nearly crying. "I am. My mum says so."

"Only as long as you don't bother anyone," Hilda Bolt hissed.

"I'm not bothering anyone," Moony said.

Hilda Bolt put her face right next to his. Her pale blue eyes filled his field of vision, the disgusting spider-smell of her choked him and her hand still tugged at his hair. Such a cold hand. So slimy. He shivered.

"You're bothering me," she said. "That's who you're bothering. Now get out of here." She pushed him through the door and turned to go back to her seat. He looked through the window at the machines. At the people. Mrs. Harding waved tentatively. Miss Clutterbuck dared to smile a little smile. Moony could see they were embarrassed. They'd never do anything. Catch them having words with Hilda Bolt. Never mind, he thought. Never mind. I've got friends they know nothing about. They'll see.

"What's this, Georgie love?" Mavis Moon picked up a piece of paper that had fallen off the table. "Is it something you did in school?"

"No," said Moony.

"When did you do it, then? It's ever so good."

"Before you came home."

"Did you copy it?"

"No."

"Looks as if you'd copied it. What's it supposed to be?"

"I dunno," Moony shrugged. "Some kind of monster."

"Not the kind of monster I'd like to meet, I'm sure," said Mavis. "Eat your beans up now. Go on."

People, Moony thought, said silly things. Even Mum. Silly. What kind of a monster *would* she like to meet, then? He looked at his drawing. It didn't look frightening to him. He said:

"I think it's quite nice. The monster, I mean. Better than a lot of people." (Spider-people. Horrible fat spider-slug people.) Mavis sighed. "Is it Hilda? She been at you again? Is that it?"

"No." Moony chased the last few beans around his plate with a fork.

"You sure now?"

"Yes." Moony had to lie. He was used to lying. If I tell the truth, he thought, she'll say I can't go in there. And I must. Must go there. That's where it is. The machine. My friend, the machine.

The Kwik and Spik closed at ten o'clock every night. Ten o'clock was Moony's bedtime. He liked the idea that he went to sleep at the same time as all the machines. He lay in his bed in the winter darkness and imagined them all, glowing faintly in the orange light of the street lamps.

I must tell it, he thought. I must tell it: not clothes. They'll take it away if it chews up the clothes. Take it and throw it on to a heap of broken old cars. Not clothes. I shall have to tell it to wait till I'm ready. Moony turned over in bed. On the floor by the chest of drawers he could see his drawing – a silver rectangle on the lino. He pushed back the blankets and got out of bed.

"You can't stay there," he said. "Go in the drawer. Go on."

He opened his bottom drawer and was just about to hide the drawing under his school socks, when something occurred to him. He looked for the pencil he'd used before, and couldn't find it. Can't go back in the other room, he thought. Mum'll see. His satchel was hanging on the chair beside his bed. He tiptoed over to it and felt around in the depths of it until his fingers found something. He looked and saw it was an orange felt-tip. That's good, he thought, orange felt-tip. Letters of fire. Moony smiled. Letters of fire sounded good. Who had said it? Where had he heard it? On the sheet of paper, next to his monster he drew a speech-bubble coming out of a face. Meant to be his face. Didn't really look like him. Never mind. A big speech bubble. Not the clothes, he thought. In the bubble he wrote:

"NOT THE CLOSE. LEEVE THE CLOSE ALOAN."

He held the paper up to the window. The orange felt tip was good. Letters of fire.

Moony slept. Breathed deeply, in and out, in and out. Below, in the Kwik and Spik launderette, the machines stood still. Dead of night. Darkness. But deep, deep in the silver entrails of one machine, a stirring, a distant rumbling, a sheathing and unsheathing of secret claws, as something breathed. Breathed deeply, in and out, just like Moony. In and out.

"Old lady been giving a bit of trouble, has she?" The first engineer was called Mike. "Let's have a look at her." He was a man with a smile for everyone, even Hilda Bolt.

"Not surprising," said the second engineer, whose name was Percy. "Been around for years, this model has. Time it was pensioned off, if you ask me."

"Hasn't been a thing wrong with it till yesterday," said Mr. Steel. "It's always given good service. Good results." He laughed nervously. "You know 'whiter than white'."

Mike and Percy had detached the offending machine from the wall, and upended it. They unscrewed the metal plates from the back, fiddled about a bit and screwed the metal plates back on again. Moony sat and watched them working, almost feeling in his own body every turn of the screwdriver, every twist and wrench of the pliers. It's like being at the dentist, he thought. Please stop. Stop it.

At last they finished and pushed the machine back against the wall.

"That should do it," Mike told Hilda Bolt. "Got anything we can try it out on?"

Hilda Bolt dug into the plastic bucket which held all the old clothes that people had dropped and neglected to claim over the months.

"Put this lot in, then," she said. "Doesn't matter what happens to them."

"Righto," Mike said and took the basket from her. Moony stood up and tapped Percy on the shoulder as he knelt in front of the machine to put the clothes in. Percy looked up.

"Please, sir," Moony said. "I've got the soap. Can I put it in? Please?"

"Go on, then," said Percy, and wandered away to speak to Mike.

Moony tipped the soap carefully into the

opening. Then he tapped softly, just above the glass door and said:

"No clothes now. Remember."

It was quite early in the morning. Mr. Steel was the only regular in the launderette. Moony was quite sure that no one had heard him. He sat in an orange chair and watched the washing going round. From time to time he thought he saw something: an eye, a flick of tail, something silvery in amongst the towels and string vests, something . . .

"Got nothing better to do, then?" Hilda Bolt was standing over him, blocking his view of the machine with her yellow nylon body.

"I just like watching it going round," Moony mumbled. Mike and Percy were still there. Moony knew she wouldn't touch him, not with them there. She went off muttering:

"Daft as a brush . . . loony bin'd be the best place for him," loud enough for Moony to hear. He felt hard lumps of hatred filling his head like stones. Wait, he said to himself. Wait and see.

The washing cycle was over. Mike opened the glass door, and Percy drew out the wet clothes.

"There you are then," they said to Hilda Bolt. "Nothing wrong with these clothes, is there? No tearing or anything."

Hilda Bolt nodded. Catch her saying thank you, Moony thought as Mike and Percy left. Probably choke her, that would, saying thank you to anyone. Probably kill her. She doesn't

16

know. Mike and Percy didn't do anything, really. She doesn't know it was me. I told it: not the clothes. It obeyed me. It's waiting, that's all. Waiting till I give the signal. And I will. When I'm ready. I will. Then she'll see.

Moony was pretending to read a comic, and listening while Miss Clutterbuck told Mrs. Harding all about her terrible experience.

"It would have to happen yesterday, wouldn't it? Just when you weren't here. Nobody was here. Only me, and I don't normally come in on a Wednesday, only my front room curtains really needed a wash, d'you know what I mean?"

Mrs. Harding nodded and looked anxiously at Miss Clutterbuck's bandaged arm.

". . . and I don't know why I used that blessed machine, anyway. I usually like the one in the window but I didn't think anything of it. I mean, the engineers were here on Saturday weren't they, after all. I knew it was working properly. And it was. Oh, yes. It washed my curtains a treat. Only afterwards – well."

"Go on," said Mrs. Harding. "What happened?"

"I don't rightly know, that's the trouble. I put my hands in to pull the curtains out. Both hands – you know what a weight wet curtains are, aren't they? Anyway, I suddenly felt the most dreadful pain, right along my arm from near the elbow right down to the wrist – terrible. I screamed, I can tell you, and pulled my arm out and it was covered in blood. Scratched myself on something, a great long horrible scratch. I thought it was a curtain hook, maybe, left in by mistake. Anyway, Mr. Rafferty was in here by then and he got the curtains out and there wasn't a single hook in them, and he felt all round the inside of the machine – nothing sharp at all." Miss Clutterbuck shook her head. "It's a mystery to me. A real mystery, but I'll tell you one thing. I'm not going near that machine again. Not ever."

"Quite right, dear," said Mrs. Harding soothingly. "Quite right."

She caught sight of Moony looking at her. "Are you all right, dear? You look very peaky."

"Yes," said Moony, "but I must go." He made for the door.

"But your Mum's not home yet, dear. Wouldn't you rather wait here?"

"I'll come back," Moony said. "I've got to do something," and he was gone, not even bothering to close the door behind him.

Moony took the picture out of the bottom drawer and looked at it carefully. I must do something, he thought. What? Poor Miss Clutterbuck. I don't want her to be scratched. I don't want anybody else to be hurt. Only Hilda Bolt. Only her. He took the drawing and sat on his bed, thinking hard. Then he found two felt tips in his satchel: black and yellow. Quickly, he drew the outline of a person and coloured it in: sour yellow. He left the face blank. No features. Instead, he carefully printed the words 'Hilda Bolt' where the nose and mouth and eyes should have been. Was that enough? Was that clear? Moony hesitated, then drew a black arrow leading from the creature's claws to the middle of the black and yellow person. That looked better, but still, not enough. He found the orange felt tip in his satchel. All the writing, he thought. All the writing in letters of fire. Along the line of the arrow leading from the claws to the yellow body he wrote: "DISTROY". Then he put the colours away, hid the drawing under his socks, and went to watch television while he waited for his mother to come home.

"I don't believe it," Moony was shouting. "I don't believe it. It isn't true."

Hilda Bolt smirked. "True as I stand here. Your mum comes in not half an hour ago, and tells me to give you this money for you to get your tea from the chippy, and also tells me to keep an eye on you till she gets back. She's going to be late, she says. Probably won't be back till closing time. So there you are. Now, stop that maithering. I don't like all this any more than you do. Go and buy your tea, and then you can sit there and keep out of my way till your mum gets here. Understand?"

"Why can't I go upstairs? To my own room?"

"And get up to goodness knows what mischief on your own? I should think not. Promised your mum, didn't I, that I'd keep an eye on you, and I can't keep it on you through the ceiling, now can I? Go on, then. Stop looking like you've seen a ghost and go and get some fish and chips or something. Go on. Scat." She turned Moony round roughly and poked a hard finger into his back.

He walked back from the chip shop in a daze. Light rain had started to fall, but Moony didn't even notice. Was tonight going to be the night he had thought about for so long? Well, maybe it was and maybe it wasn't. What if there was a crowd of people in there? He pushed open the door of the Kwik and Spik. All the machines were quiet. No one in, except for Hilda Bolt in her corner. Empty. Moony took a deep breath and sat down on the plastic chair nearest the window.

"Took your time, didn't you?" Hilda Bolt muttered without looking up. Moony didn't answer. He was staring at the machine, thinking of the letters of fire snaking along the black arrow towards the shapeless yellow person he had drawn. "DISTROY".

No one at all came in that evening. Moony watched the clock go round. Seven. Half past. Eight. Half past. At nine o'clock he looked at Hilda Bolt. The magazine had fallen out of her

20

hand, her head lolled backwards against the wall, her mouth hung open and she was snoring. Moony shivered. She would wake up. She would catch him and stop him. He was afraid of what she would do if she caught him while no one was there. But I must do it, he thought. What if someone comes in? No one must come in. I must be quick. Quick, while she's sleeping. He tiptoed over to the soap machine. The click of the money going into the slot was as loud in his ears as a gunshot. Hilda Bolt snored even louder. Moony took the soap, fed it into the top of the machine, closed the glass door, and set the dial to 'WASH'. Then he sat down again. He hadn't put any clothes into the machine. Only soap. Creamy bubbles swirled and circled against the glass. The noise filled Moony's ears. It was like a roaring, like currents of thunder rippling under black seas. Surely now, now she would wake up. He looked. She was still sleeping. The silver dial clicked round. Click, click, until it reached the point labelled 'SPIN'. That's done it, Moony thought. It's so loud now, the noise, and so fast, that she's waking up. Hilda Bolt took no longer than ten seconds to realize what was going on. Moony counted. She lumbered to her feet and came thudding towards him. Moony had never seen her so angry before. Normally he would have fled, but tonight he sat like statue, gripping the sides of the chair with white fingers. Hilda Bolt had turned purple. Her mouth was twisted into a knot, her hands shook and she was screaming at him. Her voice filled the room, rising above the noise of the machine, slicing the air, slicing like knives into Moony's ears.

"You stupid little no good dozy layabout . . . what do you think you're doing? Eh? Eh? Mucking around with these machines is forbidden, do you hear me, strictly forbidden. By the management. What do you think you're playing at, eh? Daft, loony, stupid little boy. Is it any wonder your mum's at the end of her tether? Is it? Ever asked yourself why she works so late? Eh? Have you? It's because she can't bloody stand you, that's why, and I don't blame her. If you were my kid I'd . . ."

"Stop it!" Moony had leaped to his feet. "You're horrible. It's not true. She has to work, that's all. She told me. She said. Don't dare say anything about my mum. I hate you and I wish you were dead." Moony burst into tears.

Hilda Bolt screamed with laughter.

"Think I care? Think I give a tuppenny damn what some retarded little snot-nosed brat thinks of me? You must be joking. I'll tell you something though. It's the last time you're ever coming in here. Last time you can sit and watch your precious machines going round. So there." She sniffed. "Your mum'll have to make other arrangements, that's all. Now sit down and shut your face till she gets here, d'you understand?

22

I don't want a single solitary peep out of you, or you'll feel the back of my hand."

Moony sat down, shaking all over. Hilda Bolt turned her attention to the machine.

"Bloody thing's gone mad," she shrieked. "I can't get it to stop." She drummed on the top of the machine with her fists, as if she could beat it into silence. "Stop, blast you. STOP." Drumming and drumming with her fists, kicking with her feet, red in the face and quivering with rage. Suddenly, the glass door flew open and a wave of hot water and foam rose out of the mouth of the machine nearly to the ceiling, curling round the body of Hilda Bolt, flying up into her nostrils, drenching her hair, flinging itself on to her clothes, winding itself round her limbs and sucking inexorably at her flesh: thick foam and something else. Hilda Bolt started shrieking, long, high-pitched shrieks that seemed torn out of her throat, shredding the air all around. Her arms struck out at the water, there were flashes of silver in the foam, and the noise, the roaring and the screaming and the bubbly sucking, was so loud that Moony had to cover his ears.

"What is it?" Hilda Bolt screamed over and over again. "What are you? Oh, please, please stop."

At last, after what seemed like hours (but was only three minutes by the clock on the wall) the waves and the foam subsided, the shrieking died away, the machine juddered into silence and

Moony was left alone in the Kwik and Spik launderette. There was water all over the floor and no sign of Hilda Bolt anywhere. Moony tiptoed over to the machine and feeling inside it with his hand, brought out two strips of yellow nylon that he supposed must be all that was left of her overall. But how? How was it done? Moony peered in at the silver drum, fearful of finding other bits and pieces but the drum was cool and smooth and full of neat holes. She must have been – how? – sucked through. Moony's mind swerved away from 'how'. 'How' was horrible. She was gone. Moony pushed the strips of yellow nylon into the tiny gap between the drying machine and the wall, and sat on the orange plastic chair to wait for his mother. I will say a student came in, he thought, came in and had an accident with the machine, made a flood.

"Where's Hilda?" said Moony's mother when she arrived.

"I don't know," said Moony quite truthfully.

"Well, haven't you seen her at all? She was supposed to be in charge of you, wasn't she?"

"She went out. She gave me money for my tea, but she wasn't here when I got back."

Moony's mother sighed and took the key of the launderette from its hook behind the door.

"I'm not clearing that lot up," she said, turning out the lights. "Hilda can do it when she decides to turn up. I'll lock up and that's that."

Hilda's disappearance was the talk of the Kwik and Spik for weeks. Mrs. Harding reported it. A missing person. In the first flush of excitement the Police dragged the canal, but they lost their enthusiasm after a bit, and the mystery faded from people's minds.

Moony still came in and talked to his machine, which, (all the Regulars agreed) had been washing, rinsing and spinning beautifully for weeks. The owners of the Kwik and Spik did not replace Hilda Bolt. It was hardly worth it, they felt. Not for such a small, out of the way branch.

Moony took his picture out of the drawer from time to time. As he looked at it, his ears rang with echoes of screams, and if he shut his eyes, a vision came to him of hands and claws and scales and flesh all mixed up together. The image of Hilda Bolt in his drawing had faded a little, but the orange letters still flamed on the paper and the monster he had drawn had become sleeker and more silvery, like a well-cared-for pet.

2 Live Music

April 22
Moved in. I like this street. There are lots of trees
and all the blossoms are out. The fronts of the
houses are painted white. The doors are different
colours and ours is red. There's a violin teacher
living right across the road from us, so that's
convenient. I'm going to go and have lessons
there twice a week. She's called Miss Waverley.

April 24
Miss Waverley's windows are filthy. Mum says
it's 'cos she's old and can't clean them properly,
but she seems quite healthy to me. Her garden is
overgrown and there's a grave-shaped flowerbed
in the front. Probably a pupil who always played
out of tune, ha, ha. First lesson day after
tomorrow.

April 25
Met Alan, who lives next door to Miss Waverley.
He says the sawings and scrapings of her pupils
come right through the wall of his lounge and
sometimes drown out the television programmes.
In the evenings she plays gramophone records of

famous violinists and Alan says it's just as bad and he can't tell the difference. Squealing and wailing, that's what he calls it. Alan is not very musical. He has lessons with Miss Waverley, too.

April 26
Had my first lesson. The inside of the house is not as bad as the windows, but Miss Waverley must be quite poor. Carpets are beige with all the flower pattern nearly trodden out of them. Walls were cream once but haven't been painted for years. Curtains are red velvet, but faded and worn. Miss Waverley is small and thin and very pale. Her eyes are blue with deep purple smudges underneath. I played Schubert. She just listened and when I'd finished she looked very happy. Her cheeks looked pink. She said I had talent. She said that teaching me would be a treat for her.

April 29
Had my second lesson. Did exercises. Played Schubert again. Worked on it a bit. Miss Waverley listens very hard. I've never known anyone concentrate more on listening, put more effort into it.

May 3
Violin lesson this afternoon. Later, saw Miss Waverley coming back from the shops in a beige

coat and a hat with cherries pinned on to it. Usually, she looks like a beetle, scuttling along in a black coat and a black straw hat. It must be the spring. She's looking altogether better. Pinker and healthier.

May 6
My phrasing and fingering are improving, I think. Miss Waverley is quite good at technique, but there's something odd and rather horrible about the way she listens. She sits back in her chair with her eyes closed and her mouth half open and gulps in the music with awful long shuddery breaths that make me feel scared. Sometimes I close my eyes while I play so as not to see her sitting there, but then my head is filled with a picture of the notes I'm playing sliding out like tiny black fish from the tip of my bow as I make them, and travelling through the air as though it were water. They swim into her mouth and are sucked along her veins, and when that happens I feel as if I haven't got them any more. I feel as if they've moved out of me and into her.

May 27
My technique is definitely getting better, but there's something wrong with my playing. Before I went to Miss Waverley, I had some control over what kind of sounds I could make. I had an idea of what the shape of the piece would be, of what the mood or the feel of it would be. Now, when I go for

a lesson, I feel breathless. A sort of choking feeling from the minute I get into the room.

June 7

I told Alan about Miss Waverley. I had to. I just couldn't keep it to myself any more. I hoped he'd just laugh, but he agreed with me that there was something very strange about her. He said he'd first noticed it last Christmas. They'd taken Miss Waverley to a concert, him and his parents. Alan said that she looked half dead that night. Almost as lifeless as the three staring foxes that she wore round her neck – ugh! At the concert, during the Beethoven Violin Concerto, Miss Waverley was like a child with a lolly. That's what Alan said. He said she was lapping up the music with every bit of her body. He said that what happened to Miss Waverley at the concert is what happens to Japanese paper flowers. They start out all shrivelled and dry and you can't see what colour they are, and then the moisture puffs them out into reds and pinks and sunshine yellows. They uncurl. They blossom. They grow. And that's what happened to Miss Waverley. She became all pink and plump from listening to the music. That's what Alan said.

June 9

I always make Miss Waverley a cup of tea before we begin. Alan and I call her kitchen the Black Hole of Freemont Drive, because the rhododendrons grow right up over the windows and block out the light. She sits there listening to me play and sipping her tea and it's as if she is sipping up my music at the same time. Sip, gulp, sip.

June 12
I've noticed that when I've had my lesson, I don't feel like practising afterwards. It never used to be like that. I used to rush home from lessons and I'd hardly be inside the door before starting to practise. I also used to get up early in the morning sometimes because making the music felt so good. It feels good less and less often now.

June 15
I sometimes feel like a jug that's nearly empty. The notes I play sound thin to me, but Miss Waverley is quite pleased with my progress.

June 18
Miss Waverley smiles a lot more than she did. I've felt very tired after the last couple of lessons.

June 21
Hardly feel like playing at all now, so I don't, but it makes me feel sad that I don't. It's as though someone had lopped off a part of me. Perhaps I would be O.K. with a different teacher. Would Mum agree?

June 25
Nearly fainted in the lesson today. Missed the last ten minutes. Told Miss Waverley I'd make the time up another day. She looked quite annoyed.

July 1
Asked Miss Waverley today had she ever taught someone famous. She said no, but some of her pupils might have become famous if they'd had a different teacher. I said something about maybe they weren't the right pupils, but she said no, they were just right, and she'd benefited greatly from teaching them. She smiled.

July 12
Miss Waverley looks much better than she did. The smudges under her eyes have gone and her cheeks have filled out and turned all pink.

July 15
Glory be! Mum wants me to change teachers. There's a Mr Poliansky who's very posh. You have to audition for him and he only chooses you if he thinks you're good enough. Am I still good enough? Could I be? What will Miss Waverley say? Will she be upset? I'll have to work so hard. Mum has arranged for me to see Mr. Poliansky next week.

July 20
Hurray and three cheers, he's accepted me. I couldn't believe it. He's lovely. He looks just like a violin teacher should look – tall and thin with white wavy hair and a pointy white beard. I tried so hard when I was playing for him that I nearly fell over with the effort. It was like reaching down into a tall glass jar and trying to fish a marble out of it between your fingers. It sounded pretty awful to me, but Mr. Poliansky said my technique was very good. Technically very competent, he said, and also that he thought he detected a flicker of talent in there somewhere. Now I shall have to tell Miss Waverley. Dread, dread . . .

July 21
Told Miss Waverley. She was very good about it really. Quite sad, of course, and going on about what a treat it had been for her. She called it 'a deeply satisfying experience'. Then she said: "You've given me everything you had it in you to give," or something like that. I didn't quite understand it. Then we said goodbye to one another.

August 17
Back from holiday in Scarborough. The weather was lovely. I didn't take my violin with me this time, although I've always taken it on holiday before. As soon as I got home, I played a bit of

Mozart. It sounded very rusty and mechanical to me.

August 21
Saw Miss Waverley in her garden. Said hello. Talked about the weather. The smudges are coming back under her eyes and her face looks thinner and quite pale.

August 25
Alan says Miss Waverley is wasting away. He says she lives on good music like a vampire lives on blood. She hasn't got another pupil as good as I was, so she's getting thinner and paler. I told Alan that I felt guilty, but he said I needn't feel bad about it because she'd already taken what she could from me. I said: what has she taken? and Alan said: your talent. I stormed out of the room when he said that, but I wonder if it's true? And if it's true, then will my talent ever come back? Be brought back? What will Mr. Poliansky say? Dreading my first lesson with him.

September 1
That's over and not nearly as bad as I expected. Mr. Poliansky was quite pleased with me, I think. He made me play the same section of the Beethoven six times. I saw Miss Waverley going to the shops on my way home. She is back in her long black coat again. Her face was quite white. Her skin looked like paper.

September 25
Miss Waverley died yesterday. Alan's mum and dad are going to the funeral. All the curtains in the street are pulled shut, for mourning. Alan thinks he was almost the last person to talk to her, if not the very last. He says he went round to her house with a plate of scones from his mother the evening before she died. They talked about me. Alan asked her if she was missing me, and she said she wasn't missing me at all because by the time I'd stopped going to her, my talent was almost completely used up. That's what Alan told me.

October 1
I've been thinking. If Miss Waverley was some kind of vampire, then why was she? What makes someone become like that? I've discussed it with Alan. We think maybe *she* was very talented as a child and had a teacher who sucked all the talent out of her. Then she had to use her pupils' talent to keep herself going, and in the end she needed it just to stay alive. It was like blood to her. Every bit of good music she heard was like a transfusion, and when I left and no one came to replace me, well, then she couldn't live any longer.

October 3
Have I got any talent left at all? If I have, is it

enough? Enough for me to enjoy it and be happy playing the violin? If it's not enough, or if it has all gone, then what am I going to do about it? There are only two choices: turn into another Miss Waverley, and try and exist on other people's talents, or else give up completely. I'll decide after the concert at Christmas. Mr. Poliansky isn't saying a word. He just teaches me, week in and week out, listens to me in silence and sometimes shakes his head from side to side, rather sadly.

December 17
I'm giving up the violin. I've decided. Mum will kick up a fuss but Mr. Poliansky will be on my side. I know this because I overheard him talking to someone during the concert interval last night. I know they were discussing me. Mr. Poliansky's friend said: 'A very professional technique . . . you must admit that.'

Mr. Poliansky sighed and said: 'And what use is that, eh? You tell me. For technique we have the robot music, the electronics, the synthesizers, not? Where is the heart? Where is the soul? Where, I ask you, is the *music* in that parade of so-correct notes? No, I fear she is a hopeless case. She has had the marrow and the blood sucked from the bones of the music. The sound is there but the life is gone.'

'Sucked?' his friend replied. 'How do you mean, sucked? Perhaps this child never had the music in her to begin with.'

'But she did,' Mr. Poliansky sounded sad. 'Yes, I think she did. At the end of a lesson sometimes I catch a flicker of talent, like a cloud moving over water, then it's gone. Personally, I blame her previous teacher, but what can I do? I teach and teach but I cannot put the life back into the music. Come, let us go and find coffee and gather our strength for the next half.'

So. There it is. Mr. Poliansky will support me. And I have the rest of my life to find something that will fill all the empty spaces in me where the music used to be.

3 Billy's Hand

I don't know what you've heard about Billy's hand. Everyone in the class has been so busy inventing, embroidering, twisting and magnifying what really happened that it's difficult to sort out the truth. Julia thinks, for instance, that it was a sort of collective waking nightmare brought on by the cheese in our sandwiches: I ask you! So that's what I've decided to do: tell you exactly what happened, exactly as I remember it. And I do remember it – after all, wasn't it me that Billy called for in that horrible moment? Miss Peters was there too, of course, but she's not going to give you an account of the events of that day, you can bet your boots on that. "Hysteria," she was muttering in the ambulance afterwards. "An illusion induced by hysteria." I don't know about that. I thought an illusion was something you saw that turned out to be not there at all, and you can't say that about Billy's hand, not really. But I'm jumping ahead. I mustn't do that. Back to the beginning.

Billy's hand. Doesn't it just sound like something from a horror movie? Could it be severed and dripping with blood? I'm sorry if this is a disappointment to anyone, but there are no severed heads, vampires, ghosts of the chain-rattling variety, headless horses or haunted graveyards in this story, no matter what Sharon and Tracy may have told you. What you're going to hear may be more or less terrifying, I don't know, but I can say quite truthfully that I'd rather meet a couple of thirsty vampires any day than go through that again, perhaps because vampires, etc. have become quite cosy now that we see them on T.V. such a lot.

There's another reason why I should be the one to tell the story and that's because I'm Billy's cousin. I'm not only his cousin but I live next door to him and have done all my life. And there's something else: I'm probably the only person in the world (apart from his parents) who likes Billy. The truth is, he's awful. He's a bully, the worst sort of bully, nasty and thoughtful about his unkindness, as if he spends a great deal of time working out just the right torment for the person he's getting at. I know what they say about bullies, that they're all cowards at heart and that you only have to stick up for yourself and they'll run away. Well, our Billy's not like that. He's completely fearless. Or he was completely fearless, I should say. Before that school trip, there wasn't a person on earth he wouldn't have fought, and no one he would have feared to tease or terrify, not even kids with big brothers who threatened to have him beaten up after school, or those with dads who would report him to the Head as soon as look at him.

So why do I like him? Even love him a bit, perhaps. Well, firstly, as the vampires would say, blood is thicker than water. All my life he's been there like a big brother, and no amount of remembering the gouged-out eyes of my favourite dolls, or those dreadful frogs he used to put in my bed because they were my special terror, can change that. He could always run faster, climb higher, and shout louder than me, and so he gave me something to aim for, something to copy. Secondly, he became bored of bullying me by the time we were five. We went to school together (we've been in the same class all along) and there, spread out for his pleasure, were dozens and dozens of new victims, all fresh and ready with huge buckets of tears still waiting to be shed. I learned never to cry years ago. Thirdly, when we moved up into secondary school, he became a kind of protector, sheltering me from the lesser bullies of the class. "Don't touch Kim Harrison," they used to say, "or that Billy'll get you, good and solid. She's his cousin or something." And I was grateful for this protection, and did his homework for him most nights. I also made him promise to lay off all my best friends, but sometimes he forgot. He's not very bright, except at his bullying, you see, but at that he's fiendishly clever. One day, he cut off

Shirley's thick, long plait of golden hair in the middle of a film we were watching in the school hall. It was a film about deserts, and suddenly Shirley shrieked and all the lights went on, and there was the cut-off plait under her chair, all lumpy and lifeless and horrid. I looked for Billy, but he was on the other side of the room. I'll never know how he moved so fast, nor what he did with the scissors. The Head never found out who had done it. There was no proof, though I bet he had his suspicions. Shirley cried and cried for hours all through dinner, even though it was sausages, which were her very best food of all. I screamed at Billy all the way home:

"You monster! How could you do it? I *told* you to leave Shirley alone. How could you? I'm not doing your homework for you for a month. Maybe I'll never ever do it again."

"I forgot," Billy said, smiling. "That she was your friend, I mean. Doesn't matter, it'll grow. Teach her not to be so vain."

"How come you're the one to punish everyone for their faults? Who gave you the right to teach people lessons? Brute, beast, I hate you!"

Billy didn't seem to be listening. "If you don't do my homework," he said, after some thought, "I'll clobber you so's you'll stay clobbered, know what I mean?" He winked at me.

"Clobber away, go ahead and see if I care, you bullying gasbag!" I shouted and ran ahead. I'd managed to become a bit fearless myself over the years, and at that moment I was so furious about Shirley's hair, I'd have taken on a whole army of Billys.

"Run away, go on!" he yelled after me. "Run away! GIRL! That's all you are, a silly girl. You only care about stupid Shirley's stupid old hair. You don't care about me."

It wasn't until much later, in bed, that I began to wonder if Billy was jealous of Shirley. I hadn't been playing with him nearly so much lately. It was very peculiar.

Anyway, one day we went on a class outing to the Castle, a kind of history outing it was supposed to be. We went in a coach with Miss Peters (we call her Miss Piggy because she's plump and pink, with yellow hair bouncing round her shoulders, and a really turned-up nose) and Mr. Melville, who's dry and long like a stick with hair on top, and glasses. We took packed lunches from school and ate them in a field on the way. Most people were quite glad to be out for the afternoon, it didn't really matter what the reason was, but there were a few moaners, who kept saying things like:

"Boring old pile of rubbish."

"Should've skyved off."

"Why can't they leave us here to play football and collect us on the way back?"

"Are there dungeons? I vote we lock Miss Piggy in with Old Melville!"

"I wouldn't mind so much, only they'll probably get us to write about it tomorrow. Do a project even."

We drove along a bit more after lunch, and when we first saw the Castle through the windows of the coach, everybody stopped talking. It was a very castle-like castle, square and high on top of a hill with tall, silent walls of thick, dark stone. I think Shirley was expecting a dainty turreted thing, like the Walt Disney cartoon castle in "Cinderella" or "The Sleeping Beauty".

"Gosh," she said to Miss Piggy, "it's so square and grim-looking."

Miss Piggy smiled: "Well, dear, it *is* used as a prison still, you know."

"Will we see them?" Shirley was anxious. "The prisoners, I mean?"

"No, of course not. We shall be going on the guided tour, and they're in quite another part of the buildings."

"We might hear their screams," said Billy, and shrieked with laughter.

"William Harrison, behave yourself," said Old Melville "or the screams you hear will be your own."

"What'll you do, sir, lock him in the dungeons?"

"Chain him to the wall?"

"Hang, draw and quarter him?"

"Stick his head on a spike on the castle walls?"

"SHUT UP!" I shouted, standing up in my

seat. "Don't be disgusting!" I sat down again next to Shirley.

"I think boys are revolting sometimes," I said.

"It's not just the boys," said Shirley. "Lynn was the one who suggested chaining him to the wall."

"Then girls are revolting, too. Everyone's horrible to Billy."

"Billy's pretty horrible to them, though, isn't he?"

"Yes, I know. He is. Don't let's spoil the day by talking about him. I'm looking forward to it."

"I'm not, really." Shirley sighed. "All these old things, they just don't seem real to me. I can't sort of take them seriously, know what I mean? It's as if it was a made-up story or something. I can't get worked up about things that happened donkey's years ago, not like you."

I kept quiet. I didn't admit to very many people that I found things that had happened long ago more real than a lot of the stuff that went on every day. I'd never told anyone, not even Shirley, that I couldn't go into St. Peter's Square any more without reliving the Peterloo Massacre: seeing those soldiers charging about among the terrified crowds, mothers snatching children up from under the flying hooves, men running, falling, screaming, dying. Once, we went to visit a cotton mill. I had to leave the room, pretend I was feeling sick, because I could imagine so clearly the children, no older than

43

me, sitting near the endlessly turning machines, deafened by long hours of that horrifying noise. It's not that I'm psychic or anything like that. I don't actually, physically *see* these things. It's just that I imagine them very strongly. After what happened to Billy, I asked myself over and over again whether I hadn't imagined the whole thing, but that was only to try and comfort myself, to convince myself that everything was in my own mind and nowhere else. But that's nonsense. It happened to everyone. To Billy most of all, of course, but something, something strange and something that I can't explain, happened to us all, even Miss Piggy and Old Melville.

When we got out of the coach, we went up some stone steps and waited for a while outside a small, wooden door that looked as if it hadn't been opened for centuries. But it did open, quite silently on well-oiled hinges and we went in.

The first room we saw was a courtroom, large and almost round, with high, light ceilings and a lot of heraldic shields up on the wall. The guide turned on a little silver tape-recorder and a voice spoke into the silence of all of us sitting there, listening. The voice, floating up into the carvings over the windows, told us where to go next, and we followed the real guide into a small, round high room with tall walls, like a tower. Another tape-recorder (same voice) told us all about the things we could see all round us. Lots of people perked up a bit in this room, because it was full of horrible things in glass cases, like whips and cat-o-nine-tails (or cats-o-nine-tails, do you say?) and an iron, traplike contraption called a scold's bridle, which was put over women's heads and was supposed to stop them talking too much.

"My Mum could do with that," someone said.

"What are those, sir, those kind of chains on the walls?" (These were prettily hung around, like black Christmas paper chains.)

"Neck chains," said Mr. Melville, "those big ones. And foot chains. Used to shackle people together on their way to the ships, to be deported to Australia."

Near the wall was a large wooden chair. Billy stood staring at it.

"What are you looking at that so carefully for?" I said.

"I'm trying to see how it works. It's jolly clever. You strap someone in, you see, and the more they struggle, the tighter the straps get. They used it for lunatics."

"Charming, I'm sure," I said and tried to laugh but the laughter wouldn't come. Everybody had turned quite quiet, even though the place was the opposite of gloomy. It should have been spooky, and it wasn't. It was neat, and brightly lit and quite cheerful in a peculiar kind of way. Even the dungeons, with thick stone walls and no light at all when the wooden doors were closed, were not too bad. We all took turns having the guide shut us in for a moment, and it wasn't very creepy, not with four or five others giggling and joking beside you. Miss Piggy came in with us, and Mr. Melville went with the boys. Billy looked rather pale when he came out. He wasn't talking at all.

"I think it's a bit dull," Shirley said.

"No, it must have been awful," I replied, trying to picture it in detail and failing miserably. "Think of that dark and the cold all the time, for months or years!"

"I know," said Shirley. "I know it was awful. But I can't *feel* it." I said nothing because I couldn't really feel it either, and I was worried to think that my imagination was losing its power. It was like losing your sight, in a funny kind of way.

The next room we went into was also a courtroom, and the tape-recorded voice spoke hollowly of the trials that had taken place there. A kind of double metal bracelet was fixed to the wall of the prisoner's dock, and in the olden days, people found guilty had their hands locked into the iron bands and the letter 'M' for 'Malefactor' branded on the fleshy part of their hand below the thumb. The branding-iron was still there, too. I didn't stay to look at it more carefully. Suddenly, I wanted to leave, quickly. Just for a split second, I thought I had seen him:

the Judge. Dressed in purple, or red, or black, I couldn't quite see, and he was gone almost before my imagination had pictured him there, thin, skeleton-like under the carved oak canopy above him, with eyes that could burn you deep inside more thoroughly than that hideous branding-iron in the dock. My imagination had come back with a vengeance, I thought as I hurried out. But Shirley had seen him, too. She was white.

"Did you see him?"

"Who?" (I was playing for time.)

"A man. Thin and white-faced, like a skull. He was only there for a second. Then he was gone."

"You must have imagined it." (I wasn't ready to admit anything at that stage.)

Shirley cheered up. "I'm sure I saw that man, but he can't have been real, can he, or he would have stayed put. Real people don't just vanish, do they?"

"No, of course they don't. Come on."

Shirley came, looking quite comforted. I couldn't think why. Surely she would rather have seen a real person who stayed put? Hadn't she worked out yet that if what she saw wasn't real, it could have been something else?

The room we went into (the last room we saw, as things turned out) is just a blur in my memory. I can't remember a word of the tape recording, nothing about the room at all except –

well. As soon as we were all crowded in, a shaft of sunlight came straight through the narrow window, and all of a sudden it was as if that beam of brightness was the only thing in the world. I looked and looked at it, feeling as if I was drowning in the light. While this was happening, I could feel without knowing why, that everyone else was drawn into the light, too, staring, staring and powerless to move. I vaguely remember Miss Piggy's mouth hanging open. The light faded a little, and then came the noise, so much noise that I covered my ears. There was mist now outside the window, mist everywhere, although the sun was still shining, I'm sure of that. Through the mist, I saw them. We all saw them. We talked about it afterwards. There were thousands and thousands of them: faces, people, screaming throats and waving arms, all over the castle walls. It was hard to see what they were wearing, but it wasn't modern clothes. The people were watching for something, waiting for something. I knew I didn't want to see what it was they were waiting for. I took a deep breath and made a huge effort and turned my eyes away from the window. I saw Old Melville trembling, and blinking under his thick glasses. His mouth was opening and closing and his face was getting redder and redder. It was as if he were trying to speak and nothing would come.

"Are you all right, Mr. Melville?" I said, because I honestly thought he was about to have a heart attack or something, and then two things happened.

Mr. Melville shrieked out: "For God's sake, close your eyes, oh, close them, close them now. Don't look at it! Don't look at that hideous, that hideous . . . gibbet. Oh, save these children, save them from seeing it!" He fell on his knees, crying like a first-former. Miss Piggy rushed towards him, and everyone turned to see what the commotion was about. I glanced at the window. Nothing. No people. Silence. No gallows. I was just breathing a sigh of relief when I heard Billy. Hadn't he been with us all the time?

"Kim! Kim! KIM!" The scream went right through me, into my bones. I felt so cold, I didn't know how I would move. But I ran. Faster than I've ever run before, shouting:

"Billy, Billy, I'm coming!" I could hear footsteps behind me, and Miss Piggy calling, "Wait, Kim, wait for me!"

Billy was crouched on the floor of the courtroom, clutching his hand between his knees.

"My hand!" he moaned, "Oh, Kim, look at my hand. I can't stand it, the pain, how will I ever stand it?" He was crying and crying and rolling around to try and find a way to sit that wouldn't hurt so much.

"Let me see," I said. "Come on, Billy, let me see it."

"No, no," he sobbed, "nobody must see it. Please Kim, don't look!"

"Don't be such an idiot," I said. "How can we get it better if I don't see it?"

I reached down and took Billy's hand. Under the thumb, on the fleshy part of his left hand, clear as clear, the letter 'M' was branded into the flesh: red, sore, burning. I dropped his hand in terror and turned to run away and find help. I bumped straight into Miss Piggy.

"Billy's hand is branded!" I shrieked. "It is! It is!"

"Shush, child, quiet. Sit down. Let me look at it." She sat down on a bench, and put her coat round me and went to look at Billy.

"He's fainted," she said. Mr. Melville and the others had pushed their way into the room.

"Fetch an ambulance," said Miss Piggy.

"He's been branded," I cried. "Look at his hand."

"It's hurt, certainly," said Miss Piggy. "An ugly bruise and a bad cut, that's all, but it must be very painful. I wonder how he did that?"

"It's *not* a bruise," I shouted. "It's a mark. There's the branding-iron. Touch it. Go on. Touch it."

I wouldn't touch it. I wouldn't look at the Judge's chair. I knew he would be there, the Judge. Miss Piggy and I went in the ambulance with Billy. Mr. Melville took the others back to school.

Billy's hand has a scar on it now. Just a coincidence, I suppose, that the scar happens to have the shape of an 'M'? That's the official story. They also said, the teachers and doctors, that the scar would fade. But it hasn't. Sometimes it's very pale and you can hardly see it, but sometimes it's very red and nasty. Billy rather enjoyed showing it off at first, but he never, not even to me, said a word about how he came to bear the mark in the first place.

4 The Poppycrunch Kid

"O.K, my darling, let me just explain what I want you to do, and then we'll rehearse it a couple of times before we try it on camera. Right?" Melanie nodded. Bill, the producer, was being nice to her. Much nicer than he was to everyone else in the studio. He shouted at them sometimes. Swore even, but he never shouted or swore at her, because she was the Poppycrunch Kid and Very Important. Melanie pulled her skirt down and fluffed out her bunches. Were her ribbons still all right? Mum said she was a Star. It was hard to believe. Two weeks ago, she'd lined up with a whole lot of other little girls, and they'd chosen her out of all of them to be the Poppycrunch Kid. Some of the girls had been much prettier, too.

"But your little girl, Mrs. White," Bill had said to her mother and right in front of her, too, "has such zest, such life, such – how shall I put it? Spice, that's the word, the right word – the others were all – d'you know what I mean? – flavourless. And you see, what the makers do want to promote more than anything, is an image of Brightness, Vigour and Intelligence . . .

the concept is one of Life, you see, rather than an unreal kind of prettiness. I'm sure Melanie will be Perfection Itself."

Melanie didn't understand why the sight of her trampolining, skipping, sliding down a helter-skelter, leaping out of bed or doing a tap-dance, dressed always in a red T-shirt and a short white skirt, should make everyone stop buying their favourite cereal and turn to Poppycrunch instead. She wasn't going to eat it.

"But you must," said Mrs. White in desperation.

"Why?"

"It's called Brand Loyalty. They're paying you enough money. You might at least do them the favour of eating their cereal. I think it's lovely."

"It's horrible. All hard. I could think up a few truthful slogans, like 'Tear your gums on a Poppycrunch,' or something."

"But you're going to be famous, Melanie. Don't you want to be famous? Isn't that what you've always wanted? You've said so over and over again. 'I want to be a star' you said."

"It's not being a star – not advertising cereal. I want to be in a proper show, like 'Annie'. I wish I'd got into 'Annie'."

"You were too tall. I keep telling you. And besides, millions more people see advertisements than ever walk into a theatre. Maybe someone'll spot you. You never know. Anyway, it's good exposure, you've got to say that for it."

That was the only reason Melanie could think of for doing it. Someone, someone from Hollywood even, would see her trampolining or skipping or whatever, and decide, right there on the spot, that she was exactly what he needed for his very next film, and whisk her far away in a jet to be a real actress, a child star.

"Are you ready, Melanie?" Bill cooed.

"Yes."

"Right. Let's start then."

Melanie skipped towards the trampoline (red, with 'Poppycrunch' written on it in white letters) leaped on to it and began to bounce, singing at the same time the silly little tune they'd given her to learn, and smiling widely enough to crack her face open:

> Full of goodness
> Full of fun
> Poppycrunch
> The chewy one!

Three things at once – it was harder to do than it looked, like patting your head with one hand while rubbing the other hand over your stomach in circles. Melanie had to do it four times before she'd got it just right. At last, Bill was satisfied.

"Great, my love," he said. "Absolutely scrumptious. Now as soon as you've got your breath back, we'll film it. O.K?"

"Yes," said Melanie. The thought of doing it all over again on film made the butterflies start up in her stomach, just as though she were about to act in front of a real, live audience. It was silly. There was only Bill, and Christine, his assistant and some lighting men and sound men, and her mother in the corner of the studio, and of course, the cameras. Melanie had never thought about the cameras before. They were like robots: huge square tall things on long metal legs that slid across the floor trailing thick black cables like snakes. You had to look at them quite hard to spot the men who were working them. The cameras had lenses for eyes sticking out towards you. Never, never looking at anything else except you. Melanie shivered.

"Now, Melanie, I don't want you to think about the cameras at all. Just forget about them. They're not there, all right? I want you to be quite, quite natural, my love and Reg and Ben here will do all the work – focus on you like mad, all the time. Give Melanie a little wave, lads, just to show her you're there."

Arms came out of the sides of the camera and waved. It was as if the cameras themselves were waving at her.

"Right-o, my dears," said Bill. "If you're all ready I'm going to do my Cecil B. de Mille routine . . . Roll'em!"

Melanie sang and smiled and trampolined. She sang and smiled and trampolined seven times. They had to do seven 'takes' before everything came out exactly as Bill wanted it.

"That's fantastic, Melanie. Really fantastic. It's not unknown for me to do a dozen 'takes'. Great. It's going to look great. Come and see."

Melanie went. It seemed like a lot of other advertisements to her. She was quite pleased with how high she'd managed to jump on the trampoline, but it was all over so quickly – a few seconds, that was all. Tomorrow they would do leaping out of bed. That shouldn't be so tiring. Suddenly Melanie felt exhausted, unable to think straight. The silly words and silly tune of the Poppycrunch jingle had got stuck in her head and wound round her other thoughts like thin strings of chewing-gum that wouldn't come off.

> Full of goodness
> Full of fun
> Poppycrunch
> The chewy one.

Round and round in her head.

That night, Melanie dreamed that Camera One was in her bedroom. Standing in the doorway and looking at her room. And there was a wind. It blew all round the room and sucked the furniture and the toys and all her dolls and clothes and the pictures from the walls till everything was whirling round and round in a spiral that started out huge and got smaller and smaller until at last it vanished right into the lens of the camera and then the walls weren't there any longer either, just a bed with her in it, and Camera One floating about in a bright, colourless space that went on and on for ever and never stopped.

"Christine," said Melanie, "do you think you could ask Bill something for me?"

"Of course, poppet. Anything you like. What is it?"

"Well, it's a bit embarrassing . . ."

"Go on, you can tell me. Can't you? You know I'll help."

"Yes, I know, but it's so stupid."

"Never mind, it's obviously worrying you, so go ahead and tell me. You'll feel better, honestly."

"It's Camera One. I'm scared of it."

"Scared of a camera?" Christine smiled. "But why, love? What do you think it can do to you?"

"I don't know. I dreamed about it, that's all."

"You're overwrought, my love. Don't worry. You're frightened because it's new to you. It's . . . well . . . it's a bit like stage fright, only different. Come and have a look. I'll get Reg to let you touch it and get to know it so you'll never be frightened of it again."

Reg was understanding.

"It's only a kind of mechanical eye, love. That's all. Metal and glass and stuff that can see. It is a bit like magic, I grant you, because it's a clever old thing. Does a lot that your eyes and mine can't do – it can give back the pictures that it sees and show them all over again, but it's not magic, see. It's called Technology. Nothing to be scared of, honestly."

"No, I suppose not," said Melanie. "I'm being stupid."

"No, no love," said Reg. "It's not stupid. I'll tell you something. There are primitive tribes in the world, New Guinea and places like that, and they don't even like snapshots being taken of them. They reckon every time a photo gets taken, it steals away a bit of their soul. That's their superstition, see? Bet you've had a million snapshots taken of you since you were born, and you're none the worse for it, are you? Neither is anyone else. So don't worry, O.K?"

"O.K," said Melanie and went over to the beautiful bed that had been set out on the studio floor. I wish Reg hadn't told me that, she thought. About those people in New Guinea. I know it's only a superstition, but I wish he hadn't told me, all the same.

"Action!" Bill shouted and Melanie bounded out of bed, grinning and singing:

> Ready for work
> Ready for play.
> Start every day
> The Poppycrunch way!

She did it ten times. It wasn't her fault. They

had to find some way of getting the pillow into the picture with her. The famous Poppycrunch symbol was printed on the pillowslip, and of course, it had to be seen, or what was the point?

There were three more films to make. The helter-skelter was fun. A very short tune and not a lot of words:

> Bite it
> Munch it
> Poppycrunch it!

Also, Melanie didn't care how many times she had to come sliding down till the timing was just perfect. She was getting used to filming, beginning to enjoy it, just as Bill and Christine and Reg had said she would. She sang the songs at home, all the time. At school, she showed her friends exactly what she had to do. She found it very hard to concentrate on her work, because her head was full of bouncy music and bright slogan words and they seemed to be pushing whatever it was she was supposed to be thinking about into some corner of her mind where she could never quite reach it. Miss Hathersage, her teacher, asked her one day:

"Melanie, dear, what are seven nines?"

Melanie's mind raced. Seven nines? What were nines? Full of goodness . . . Nine whats? Sevens . . . Full of fun . . .

"I don't know, please, Miss."

"Of course you know, dear. You did the

nine times table last year. Now come on, dear, think."

Melanie thought . . . the chewy one. She closed her eyes . . . white skirt flying . . . jump as high as you can . . . Poppycrunch . . . ready for work . . . ready for play . . .

"I can't think, Miss, I'm sorry." Melanie hung her head.

"Very well, then. Sarah, some people have let being on television go to their heads, I can see. What are seven nines?"

"Sixty three, Miss Hathersage."

"Quite right. Sixty three. Do you remember now, Melanie?"

"Yes, Miss." But I don't remember, Melanie thought. I don't and I must. Seven nines are sixty three, sixty three. Even as she thought it, she felt the numbers slipping away, losing their meaning, losing themselves over the precipices that seemed to lie at the very edges of her mind.

That night, Melanie dreamed that she was reading. Camera One was looking at her as she turned the pages of her book. She watched as the words flew off the page and drifted on to the floor, millions of tiny black letters, all over the rug. She tried to pick them up and put them back into the book in the right order, but they fell out of her hands, and crumbled like ash when she touched them.

"What's the matter, love?" said Christine. "You're looking a bit pale today. Are you tired? I bet you are, you know. You've had to do all these films one on top of the other, and never a rest in between. Bill," she raised her voice. "I'm going to take Melanie back to Make-Up. I think she needs a spot more rouge, don't you?"

Bill came and stood in front of Melanie, frowning.

"Yes, darling. Oh, and ask them at the same time to see if they can get rid of those shadows under her eyes. You've not been looking after yourself, love, now have you? You must, you know. That's what we're paying you for – to look healthy, full of life. Run along with Christine now and see what Make-Up can do for you."

Melanie lay in the make-up chair listening to Christine's voice which seemed to come from very far away.

"I don't think you're getting enough sleep, love. Honestly. Are you?"

"I start every day the Poppycrunch way . . ." Melanie whispered.

"Are you sleeping properly, Melanie?"

"I dream a lot," Melanie said.

"Bad dreams?" Christine sounded concerned.

"No. Poppycrunch dreams. Just me and Camera One."

"You dream about Camera One? I thought

you'd got over all that. You don't seem nervous in front of the cameras at all. What do you dream?"

"I dream I'm singing and I don't know what comes next and then Camera One looks at me and I know . . . I know what to do if it looks at me. It tells me what to say."

"What does it tell you to say?"

"Words. Tunes.

> Poppycrunch for you
> Poppycrunch for me
> Poppycrunch for breakfast
> Poppycrunch for tea."

"Those are today's words," Christine sounded worried. "I'll have a word with your Mum and Bill after the filming today. I reckon you need a damn good rest. You're just exhausted. Tell me," she added as though something had just occurred to her, "what do you do at home? For relaxation? Do you read any books?"

"No. I stopped. I used to like it, but then I stopped."

"Why did you stop?"

Melanie looked up. "Because I can't remember what the story's about any more. I can't hold the story in my head. It's as though," Melanie hesitated, "as though my head's full of deep, black water and everything that goes in it just sinks under the water and won't come up to the surface again."

"Right," said Christine. "See if you can get

through this afternoon's filming and then I'll have a word with them. It won't be long now."

"Oh," Melanie's face lit up, "you don't have to do that. Don't worry. I love it. I love the filming. I love Camera One. I know all the words. And all the tunes. And just what to do." Melanie skipped all the way back to the studio, singing the Poppycrunch jingle for today. Christine followed more slowly. All hell was going to break loose when she told Bill. That was for sure.

"Christine, my beloved," said Bill, "you have clearly taken leave of your senses. Let me go over what you've just said. Melanie White is exhausted and overwrought and you think we should scrap the whole of the last film. Is that right?"

"Yes," said Christine quietly. "That's quite right."

"Well, now, I'll answer you as calmly as I can because I don't want a row. I'll try and go over the points one by one so that you understand. First, the Poppycrunch commercials are the hottest thing I've done since the Suckamints Campaign, and you know how many prizes that won. Sales of Poppycrunch are up twenty per cent in the last two weeks. It follows, therefore, that the makers are not going to look kindly on someone jeopardizing their profits. Second, this last film is the biggest and most important of all. It's much longer. It's got fifteen other kids in it besides Melanie, doing things in the background while she dances at the front, and each one of those kids has to be cossetted and looked after, not to mention paid. It has a ten-piece band that has to be cossetted and looked after as much as the kids and paid even more. We've booked studio time. We've rehearsed, and we've even paid through our noses to be allowed to use the tune of 'Sweet Georgia Brown'. So I ask you, how can I cancel? Go on. Tell me. I'm anxious to know."

Christine said nothing. Bill went on:

"What do you think, Mrs. White? Would you be in favour of cancelling? Do you think Melanie is exhausted and overwrought?"

"Well," Mrs. White considered. "She is a bit tired, naturally. I mean, we all are, aren't we? I am myself and I just sit here and watch. But Melanie would be ever so put out if it was cancelled. I do know that. Eats, drinks and sleeps Poppycrunch, she does. Obsessed with it. Sings those tunes all day and every day. If her friends come over she teaches them all the words, tells them everything she has to do. They just play Poppycrunch games. Well, they don't come round much any more. I reckon they're fed up and I have said to her she ought to ease up a bit, but it's as if she can't. It's as if, I can't explain it really, as if there's no room left inside her for anything else."

"Then don't you think we should stop it before it's too late?" Christine said. "You're her mother. You can see. You've said yourself – she's obsessed."

"Yes, but," Mrs. White looked down at her hands, embarrassed, "I'm sure it'll be all right when all the filming's finished. It is only one more after all, isn't it?"

"Right," said Bill. "Only one more. So that's decided. I'm really glad we were able to agree, Mrs. White. It's going to be a corker, this last film. Wait and see."

That night, Melanie dreamed again. Her mother, and her school friends and Bill and Christine were all standing in the television studio and one by one they went up and stood in front of Camera One. Each one of them went right up to the camera and said something and then they got smaller and smaller until they disappeared altogether. Then she went and stood right up close to Camera One and said 'I'm the Poppycrunch Kid' and then she got larger and larger until she took up all the space in the studio and Camera One kept looking at her and she kept growing and growing until she was all there was left in the whole world.

Melanie knew all the words, of course, but they were written up on a big board for the benefit of the fifteen little girls who had to jiggle up and down in the background while Melanie tap-danced at the front. The only words Melanie had to sing were: 'The Poppycrunch Kid'. She had to sing it six times and then the film ended with her singing the last three lines all on her own. This is the best of all, thought Melanie. A real band, not a tape, all those other children, and that tune, so much more zingy than the others.

"Here we go, kids," said Bill. "Let's try it from the top."

The saxophone played an introduction and the children dutifully began jigging about and singing as Melanie went into the dance routine:

"Who's that kid with the bouncy step?"
"The Poppycrunch Kid!"
   (this was Melanie's line.)
"Who's the girl who's full of pep?"
"The Poppycrunch Kid!"
"Who's got the other kids all sewn up?"
"The Poppycrunch Kid!"
"The Poppycrunch Kid!"
"You said it, you did!"

"Who's got the shiny eyes and hair?"
"The Poppycrunch Kid!"
"When fun happens, who's right there?"
"The Poppycrunch Kid!"
"The cereal this kid eats
Is the kind with the built-in treats . . .
Nuts and honey
For your money
Be a Poppycrunch Kid!"

It was much harder, Melanie decided, filming with all the others. So many things went wrong. Someone's hair ribbon coming undone, someone looking the wrong way, a wrong note from one of the band: any one of a thousand things could happen and did happen and they had to start again. Melanie didn't mind. She fixed her eyes on Camera One's magic eye, and felt as though just looking at it, she was falling and falling down into a place where there was nothing except light and music and tapping feet and words that circled in her brain and didn't puzzle her or worry her or make her think: words that comforted her, made her feel safe, magic words that were all she needed to say. Spells, incantations that were so powerful they could empty your head of every other thought . . .

"Twenty takes," said Bill. "I'm finished. Completely and utterly finished, Christine, and that's the truth."

"You're not the only one," said Christine. "Did you see Melanie?"

"She's a real trouper, that kid. I mean she even looked as if she were loving every minute of it all the way through."

"She was," said Christine. "It's not normal. How's she going to go back to ordinary life? I worry about it sometimes."

"Don't be silly, love. It's not as though she's

the first child ever to appear on a commercial.
We've got another lot coming in tomorrow to
audition for the crisps film, Lord help us."

"No, but she was different."

"Bloody good on camera, though," said Bill,
"and that's what counts in the end, isn't it?"

"Oh yes," Christine agreed dully. "The
camera just loved her. You could see that."

On the studio floor, Camera One stood amid
its cables with a plastic cover over it to protect it
from the dust. Its work was finished. Until
tomorrow. Until the next child was chosen.

"Hello, dear," said the doctor. "And how are
you today?"

"Full of goodness, full of fun," said Melanie.

"You're looking much better, I must say.
Have you thought about what I asked you
yesterday?"

Melanie nodded.

"Good girl. That's a good girl. Now. Tell me
who you are. Tell me your name."

"The Poppycrunch Kid."

"No, Melanie. That's not your name, is it?
Your name is Melanie White. Believe me. Say
it."

"Melanie White."

"There, doesn't that sound better? Are you
going to play today, Melanie?"

"Ready for work, ready for play, start every
day the Poppycrunch way."

"You could play outside today. It's a beautiful day."

"I'm full of pep . . ."

"I'm glad to hear it. Your mother will be coming to see you today. That'll be nice, won't it? You love having visitors, don't you?"

"Bite it, munch it, Poppycrunch it . . ."

"I'll see you tomorrow then, Melanie." The doctor stood up. "I'll look in after breakfast."

"Poppycrunch for breakfast," said Melanie and turned over to look at the wall.

I've got shiny eyes and hair and when fun happens I'm right there, but they took Camera One away. Maybe if I'm extra good, it'll come back. I'm the kid with the bouncy step. That man. He's the producer. But I've got the other kids all sewn up. They can't let anyone else be the Poppycrunch Kid. They put me here to see. To see if I really am the Poppycrunch Kid and if I'm not, then they'll choose someone else. But I'm the one – The Poppycrunch Kid, you said it, you did – when fun happens who's right there, the cereal this kid eats, is the one with the built-in treats, nuts and honey, bite it, munch it, Poppycrunch it.

She could hear them at visiting time.

"Look, Herbert," said the lady's voice. "Isn't that the kid who was on the telly? You know, that Poppycereal stuff. I'm sure it's her."

"Don't be silly," said Herbert. "She was

pretty – full of life. That kid looks half dead to
me."

I'm not, she thought, I'm full of fun, full of
goodness . . . Poppycrunch for me . . .

5 Mirror

"Thought I'd put you in here for a change," said Aunt Lawrence. "The spare room's under about six feet of my maps and papers and things and you know me – don't like clearing up unless I have to."

"That's all right," said Josie, smiling. "We don't mind, do we Bel? This room's great."

"It's lovely," said Bel, standing at the window beside the dressing-table. "I can see the sea, over there, beyond the trees."

"I'll let you get on then, with your unpacking and what have you, and I'll see you for tea in the kitchen, what? In half an hour? That suit you?"

The girls nodded and Aunt Lawrence left the room. The stairs squeaked under the weight of her stout, tweedy body, her heavy, lace-up shoes. Josie thought suddenly of her great-aunt's dressing-gown: grey and brown checks, thick and woollen even in the summer, and of her slippers, sensible brown leather. "I don't believe in summer," Aunt Lawrence often said. "It's a figment of the ice-cream manufacturers' imaginations."

"We've never been here in the summer

before," Josie said. "Chimneys seems such a wintery house."

"It's the sea, I expect," said Bel, still standing at the window. "The mist rolls in from the sea and there's all that rain always but you can see it's summer. All the leaves are out. And look, there's Ozzy lying on that bench round the apple tree. He'd never go out if it wasn't summer. Oh, come on Josie, let's hurry up and unpack. I do want to go down and stroke him."

Josie began putting her T-shirts carefully into a drawer. "You're daft about that cat. He's not a stroking kind of cat at all. He's fat and bad-tempered and his fur falls out."

"It does not." Bel dreamily let clothes fall into her drawer like leaves from a tree – haphazardly. "He's just moulting, that's all. I love him."

"You'd love anything," said Josie, "as long as it had fur or feathers or scales or slimy skin. You're animal-mad." She made a mental note of the fact that her sister's drawer was a mess, and not only was she not going to tidy it this time, as she always did at home, she was going to make a huge effort not even to care, not even to think about it. Bel had finished unpacking. Well, thought Josie, it doesn't take long when all you do is tip the clothes from one container to another. She was now sitting on the dressing-table stool, looking into the mirror.

"Look at this, Josie, there's about a thousand different views of your face. Front, sides, even the back almost, if you move this bit over to the right a little."

Josie looked at her sister in the wing mirror: her full face in the middle and thin slices of her profile reflected on the silver all around.

"Your hair's a bit of a mess," said Josie absently, but she was struck, as she always was when she was forced to think about it, by Bel's pale prettiness, the light blue of her eyes and her wide brow under the silvery blonde hair. She looked into the mirror herself. Not a bad sort of face, she thought. A good everyday face. Brown plaits and straight brown eyebrows over big, brown eyes. "We don't look like sisters at all," she said. "Luckily for you."

Bel wasn't listening. She seemed fascinated by the mirror, moving the wings this way and that, trying to catch different parts of the room within the boundaries of the glass: the twin beds covered with maroon candlewick, the carved oak cupboard in the far corner, the flower-patterned carpet, and the tiny chandelier that hung from the centre of the ceiling and produced a host of little lights to twinkle round her hair like a crown of stars.

"I'm going down now," said Josie. "Are you coming?"

"In a second," said Bel. "I ought to comb my hair, oughtn't I?"

"Yes, O.K." said Josie. "D'you want me to wait for you?"

"No, it's all right. I'll be down when I've done this." She picked up a brush, backed in silver. "This is posh, isn't it? Can we use it, do you think?"

"I expect so," said Josie. She hesitated by the door and looked at Bel. At the back of her head, which was her, and at her face, which was only an image of her. As she turned away, it seemed to Josie that there was another face in the glass. She had a sudden powerful impression of long, black hair, a strong profile, very near her sister's, sharing the mirror with her. She strode over to the dressing-table and looked closely at every image of Bel that she could see. Her own face stared back at her. I look angry, she thought.

"What's the matter?" asked Bel.

"Nothing. I thought I saw someone else in that mirror, just as I was going out of the room."

"But there is no one else, silly. Only you and me."

"Yes," said Josie. "I know. Of course there's no one else."

Nevertheless, she waited until Bel had brushed her hair and they left the room together.

"Where's Isabel?" said Aunt Lawrence, washing dishes in the stone sink with great gusto and sliding them into Josie's outstretched hands to be dried with all the flourish of a circus juggler.

"Probably gone to look for Ozzy."

"Loves animals, doesn't she?" Aunt Lawrence

chuckled. "It's funny, you know, but I always think of you as the elder sister, even though you're two years younger."

"It's because I'm taller."

"No," Aunt Lawrence considered. "Not only that. Dear Isabel is so impractical. So dreamy. Poetic, some'd call her. Writes poetry too, doesn't she?"

"Well, I think so," Josie said. "She doesn't like anyone to know really. I promised I wouldn't tell."

"Sticks out a mile," Aunt Lawrence said. "Don't worry, though, I shan't breathe a word. She's like Martin of course, and you're like your mother. Extraordinary thing, genetics. I should have liked to go into all that. Never had the time. Perhaps when I retire. There. That's the dishes done. Now I can just catch the headlines on television." She hurried out of the room.

Aunt Lawrence was the girls' father's aunt, their great-aunt, in fact, though she would not allow the words to be spoken because they made her feel old. She taught history and geography at the local school, cycling to and from work each day through the fields, over the silent ribbons of roads, her face flushed, her longish grey hair streaming behind her, encased in a royal blue cagoule when the weather was wet and in a khaki corduroy jacket when it was fine. Her mind was as orderly and swift as a computer. You had only to ask the right question and out would come data: all the data you could wish for on anything from fossils to farthingales, from rock formations to Rockingham china. Her house, however, was a swirling mess of old newspapers, books, maps, stones, shells, pieces of driftwood through which she moved like a barge moving through the flotsam and jetsam of a river. Underneath the mess, Josie could see glimpses of good solid furniture, well-upholstered chairs, wool carpets, splendid antique table lamps, delicate water-colours on the wall, bone china tea cups, copper saucepans, all peeping out from the tidal wave of chaos that surrounded Aunt Lawrence wherever she went. Josie was tidy. In her own room, in her own life, untidiness was something she fought against, something she hated. Bel was dreadful about putting her clothes away and Josie had long ago decided that if she wanted their room to look decent, she would have to do the tidying, and she did, without complaint. She also saw to it that Bel was up in good time for school, did her homework, remembered to put her underwear in the laundry basket. In fact, she thought, as she wiped a cloth over the pine table, and tried to find space on a crowded shelf for the salt cellar, I look after her. Just like an older sister.

Josie had often thought about this and had realised three things, not one of which she would have confided to anyone. Firstly, she loved her sister, even though she knew that this was most unfashionable and that all her friends at school denied vehemently having feelings of affection for their siblings, and daily reported rows, fights and quarrels of astounding ferocity and nastiness. Secondly, she admired Bel. Bel could sew: little animals out of felt, clothes for dolls when they were younger, anything. She could knit and embroider. She had a beautiful singing voice and told wonderful stories in bed at night. Animals loved her. So did little children. And Bel was pretty, like a princess in a fairy tale. Josie knew very well the dangers of judging a book by its cover, knew that beauty could be a mask sometimes, but still, it was hard not to admire it; particularly when you knew that the beautiful person was also kind, loving and generous. It isn't either, Josie thought, that I'm totally untalented and ugly. There's plenty of things I can do that Bel never could, but the things other people can do always seem better, cleverer in some way than the things you can do yourself. Most of all, most secret of all was the feeling of protectiveness Bel aroused in Josie. Josie had sensed from a very early age that her sister was fragile in some way and she had set herself to be the one that guarded her. Exactly how she was fragile had not yet become clear. Bel's health was excellent in spite of her delicate looks, and so far there had been nothing remotely threatening in her life, either at home or at school, but Josie felt protective, all the same. This evening, as Bel had sat at the mirror, fear for her safety, a desire to pull her away from some danger had been very strong, just for a second. Almost overwhelming.

"I'm going soft in the head," Josie said aloud. "It must be all this sea mist and creaking old stairs and rustling trees." Bel came into the kitchen, carrying Ozzy, who, if he hated being cuddled and petted, was at least putting up with it quietly.

"Hello," said Josie. "Are you coming to play Scrabble?"

"Yes, I will for a bit. But I'm tired. Aren't you tired?"

"Not really. Well, a little, I suppose, but only from the train journey. Anyway, I like playing Scrabble with Aunt Lawrence. She puts down words you've never even heard of."

Bel left the Scrabble game early. Josie and Aunt Lawrence played on.

"Aunt Lawrence," Josie said suddenly. "Do you think Bel is a fragile sort of person?"

Aunt Lawrence considered the question seriously, as she considered every question. Finally she said: "I don't think I'd say fragile exactly. Impressionable is the word I'd choose."

"What does that mean exactly?"

"Imagine a piece of soft wax. If you press a coin down onto it, the pattern on the coin will be imprinted quite easily on the wax. That's what I mean. All kinds of things will leave their mark on her. Still, I suppose that's not altogether bad."

"I suppose not," said Josie softly.

Aunt Lawrence won the game as she always did and Josie put the tiles away in their bag.

"Good night, Aunt Lawrence," she said.

"Good night, dear. Jolly nice having you girls to stay in the summer for a change. I think your parents ought to go off to America for conferences more often."

Josie smiled.

"It's very good of you to have us," she said.

"My pleasure," said Aunt Lawrence.

"Thought you'd be in bed by now," said Josie as she came into the room. "Whatever are you doing?" Bel was at the dressing-table.

"Nothing. Just looking at myself, that's all."

"Vain."

"Not really. But I like this mirror."

"I can see that. You're not going to sit there all night, are you?"

"No, of course not," said Bel, and rose reluctantly from the stool.

Damn and blast, thought Josie as the first light of dawn fell on to her pillow. I forgot to pull the curtains across last night. I'd better do it now and try and get back to sleep. She looked at her watch. Five o'clock. The middle of the night. Softly, so as not to wake Bel, she tiptoed across the room to the window. The dark green curtains made a small scraping noise as she pulled them shut. Bel stirred in her sleep. There, that's better, thought Josie. Not completely dark, but better. Like being under the sea. Watery grey light. Not even half light. A furry kind of dimness. I've gone and woken myself up properly now, she thought in despair. I'm not a bit sleepy. What on earth am I going to do until eight o'clock? That's three whole hours. Josie sat down at the dressing table and looked into the mirror, pondering. She could make a cup of tea, walk in the garden, read a book in the kitchen . . . and then her heart stopped. There was another face in the mirror alongside hers. Josie tried to close her eyes and found they wouldn't close. She tried to put her hands up in front of her face to shield her from that other face, and her hands had lost their power to move. She called out to Bel, but the call was silent, stuck in her throat. And still the face was there. Josie sat and looked, mesmerised. It was a woman's face. A long fall of black curls, a white skin, and dark, laughing eyes, a smiling mouth too, but not a happy smile. A disdainful, scornful smile. Evil. Josie pulled herself away from the dressing-table and lay shivering in her bed with the sheets drawn up round her head, waiting for eight o'clock. Waiting for Bel to wake up. And Aunt Lawrence. Waiting for breakfast. Real life. That, that creature in the mirror couldn't have been real. Must have been a dream. Josie knew that she had seen it, that it had not been a dream, and yet she comforted herself: quite often when we're dreaming we're quite sure it's real. Until we wake up. I wish, she thought, if it is a dream, I wish I could wake up now.

"Bel, can I ask you something?" The girls were sitting on the beach, letting small waves curl up around their toes. The sand was damp still from the rain that had fallen that morning and the sky was streaked with cloud. Bel nodded.

"Have you ever seen anyone in that mirror? Anyone besides us, I mean."

"No, of course I haven't. Don't be so childish," said Bel and stood up. "Come on. Let's go in now. I find this beach unbelievably tedious." She started to walk towards the cliff path.

Josie blinked the tears away and stared fixedly at the horizon. Bel had spoken so sharply. Surely there was no need to be so . . . angry. And what had she said? That the beach was 'unbelievably tedious'. That wasn't the kind of thing Bel said. Bel loved the beach. Didn't she? Why was she so different? Josie decided finally that something must be worrying her. I'll keep a sharp eye open, she thought. She'll have to tell me. And even if she doesn't, I'll find out.

A cold, wet summer. For days on end the rain fell, surrounding Chimneys in blue drizzle. The sea vanished behind a curtain of mist and the trees stood dripping on to the sodden lawns. Bel spent many hours in the bedroom. In front of the mirror. Josie covered up for her – told Aunt Lawrence she was reading – and Aunt Lawrence simply nodded and never asked why Bel couldn't read in the lounge or the kitchen, or the study. A terrible change had come over her elder sister, Josie was convinced of it. She couldn't explain, but she knew it was connected with the wing mirror upstairs. Bel seemed almost bewitched by it, although she denied ever having seen anything reflected there other than her own face and the room behind her.

And then, one evening, the rain cleared from the west and the sky over the horizon shone like pearls.

"Enough of this skulking indoors," said Aunt Lawrence. "We may not get an evening like this for another week. Let's walk down to Flint's End. Are you coming, Bel?"

She'll say no, Josie thought. She says no to everything now.

"Yes, I'll come," said Bel and went upstairs to fetch her cardigan.

They walked slowly along the cliff path for more than a mile. Bel and Aunt Lawrence walked a little ahead of Josie who watched Bel carefully. It was dreadful to know someone so well that you noticed every tiny thing about them. Bel was walking differently, Josie could see. Swishing along in a grown-up sort of way, almost as though she had high-heeled shoes on. If I were to tell anyone, Josie thought, they'd laugh at me. They wouldn't even know what I meant. Perhaps she's only pretending. Pretending to be a lady. Or something. Anyway, we're out of that house. Away from the mirror. In the air. There isn't anything bad here. She looked back along the path. Chimneys in the distance stood out against the pale sky like a silhouette: a pointed roof, beside pointed trees – a storybook house.

"Come and have a look at these rocks," Aunt Lawrence shouted and Josie turned and ran up to her. "Look down there," said Aunt Lawrence, "but keep away from the edge. We've already had one fatality here this year."

"Really?" Josie's mouth fell open. "Was it anyone you knew?"

"Well, I'd seen her, of course. Poor little thing. Didn't know her though. Not really."

"Was it a child?"

"Oh, no. Nothing like that."

"Do tell us," Josie begged. Bel said nothing. She was gazing down into the black water, looking at the ragged edges of foam scraping against the raw grey sharpness of the rocks. She was smiling.

"Bel," Josie called. "Come and listen."

"I can hear," Bel replied coolly. "I can hear everything."

Aunt Lawrence sat down, was silent for a

moment, looking out to sea. The water sucked and ground and wailed around the boulders.

"Well," Aunt Lawrence began, "there's nothing much to tell. A lot of it is hearsay anyway and you know me, I don't believe anything at all without solid scientific proof, much less anything about ghosts."

Josie settled herself more comfortably beside Aunt Lawrence.

"Are there ghosts in the story? Lovely. I thought it was just a sad story."

"Well now. A man called Mr. Richard Daley came to live here about five years ago. He was reasonably wealthy. Brought his wife with him, down from London. I never saw her, of course, but they say she was very beautiful. Claire, her name was. She was very smart. Sophisticated, I suppose would be the word. She was also rather proud and difficult. High-handed. Threw her weight around. Got up the noses of the locals, do you know what I mean?"

Josie nodded.

"She was insanely jealous and not above a childish tantrum. Poor Mr. Daley had only to exchange a few words with someone and, well, Claire once scratched a barmaid's face with her bare hands, so they say, just for sharing a joke with Mr. Daley in a crowded Saloon Bar. Anyway, where was I?"

"She was jealous. And nasty," Josie said eagerly.

"Precisely. Well, all that came to an end rather suddenly about six months ago. Claire Daley was killed in a car accident, poor thing. Fought tooth and nail in hospital to hang on to life, they said, but death took her in the end."

"Is that it?"

"No, no not at all. Mr. Daley married his secretary, Margaret. A pretty blonde, slip of a thing. They married about two months after Claire died and, about six weeks after the wedding, the second Mrs. Daley's body was found down there on those rocks."

"That's awful. But why did you say it was a ghost story?"

"I never said anything of the kind. The ghostly part was put about by some of my children at school. They seemed to think that Claire carried her jealousy with her beyond the grave, and haunted poor little Margaret into such a state that she simply had to put an end to her life. Down there."

Josie shivered.

"Does Mr. Daley still live here? It must be horrible for him."

"Oh, no, he's gone back to London. Sold the house with all its contents and left. I went to the sale, as a matter of fact. That wing mirror in the room you're in, that came from the house."

Aunt Lawrence stood up and brushed grass from her skirt. "We should be making for home now, I think, don't you?"

Josie walked towards Chimneys in silence. I know everything now, she thought. I know who it is now. Who Bel is becoming. I must warn her. Tonight. I must help her.

It was nearly dark by the time they reached Chimneys. Josie stepped into the hall first and held the door open for her sister. Bel said nothing as she came in, but even in the half light, Josie could see the smile, no, the smirk, that twisted up the corners of her mouth.

Two more days to go, Josie thought as she made her way upstairs. Only two more days and we shall be away from her. Away from that room with the mirror, away from everything. Ozzy came up the stairs behind her. She opened the door. Bel was sitting at the dressing table, brushing her hair.

"You might close the door behind you," she said coldly. Bel never said things like that. It wasn't Bel talking. Josie closed the door and went to sit on her bed. Ozzy went up to Bel at the dressing table and started to rub himself against her leg. Bel stiffened, then reached down and grabbed him roughly round the stomach in hands that seemed to be made of steel and flung him as hard as she could towards the chest of drawers. Ozzy ran for the nearest bed and cowered under it. Josie sprang to her feet.

"What're you doing, Bel? It's Ozzy."

"Ozzy?" Bel smiled. "Stupid name. Horrid

smelly fat creature. Why don't you keep him away from me? Don't you know I hate cats? Well, don't you?"

Josie burst into tears.

"It's not true," she shrieked. "You don't hate them. You love them. All animals."

"Stop shrieking at me. What are you talking about? I really can't think what's got into you."

Josie stood beside her sister, trembling.

"It's you. Can't you see? Something's got into you. Someone has. It's her. Claire Daley. I see her in the mirror. You say you don't see her. I don't know if I believe you or not, but she's there, and she's taken you, Bel, and turned you into her. She didn't want to die. Aunt Lawrence said. She fought with death and now she sees the chance of a second life through you, so she's got into you. Oh, Bel, how will I ever get her out?"

"I've never heard such nonsense in my whole life," said Bel, calmly.

"It's not, it's not, look," and Josie pushed her sister's face up close to the glass. "Can't you see her? She's there. Oh look, look, Bel. She's laughing at you. Can't you see?"

Bel laughed too, and her smile matched the mocking smile in the mirror. Her blue eyes reflected the coldness of the black eyes in the glass.

"I'm not going to let this happen," Josie

whispered, and she picked up the silver-backed brush and smashed it against the mirror with all her strength. Bel staggered back from the dressing-table with a terrible moaning sobbing cry as though it were she who was being attacked, hit, destroyed. Josie went on and on, smashing the brush down on to the glass again and again until fragments of the dark, laughing face lay scattered in tiny slivers of light around her feet. Then Aunt Lawrence came into the room, and Josie fainted, the hairbrush still in her hand.

The memory was beginning to fade. Sometimes at night, Josie could still feel the full horror of it all: Bel's illness, Bel in hospital, Bel nearly dying . . . of what? Something. The doctors didn't understand, but Josie did. Bel nearly died because something that had been part of her had been wrenched away, torn out, uprooted from within her. And she, Josie, had done that. Why, she asked herself many times, why didn't I smash that mirror on the very first day, before that creature had the time to embed herself in my sister, imprint herself, just as Aunt Lawrence had said, on Bel like a coin on warm wax? I should have done it the instant I saw her. And then none of this would have happened: the worry to Aunt Lawrence, who couldn't think what had happened, either to her great-nieces or, indeed, to her mirror, going home in an ambulance, her parents driving straight from the airport to the hospital bed of their daughter. If only I'd been a little quicker. But still, the worst part was over. Bel would be all right. She would be coming back tomorrow. She was almost herself again. It seemed to Josie, who had sat for hours at her sister's bedside, that Bel had, she didn't know how to describe it exactly, faded a little. She was a quieter, smaller, paler, more soft spoken version of herself. It was exactly as though a little bit of her had been eroded, rubbed away by Claire Daley's strong, abrasive personality. It was as if harbouring such a character in her body for a short while had flattened a little of Bel's real self. Josie shook her head. It's nonsense. She's probably just weak. It'll take time for her to get back to what she was, that's all. It was easy to be optimistic at home. Easy to think happy thoughts in this new, white-painted tidy little house, set in a street of other white-painted tidy little houses just like it. So simple, in the streamlined kitchen, washing dishes in a double-drainer stainless steel sink, walking on wall-to-wall carpets, to take everything and push it to the back of the mind.

Bel was coming back tomorrow. Her parents had taken a case full of clothes to the hospital. Josie was alone in the house. She looked at the kitchen table and thought, "What's a vase of sweet peas doing there? We don't need them in here. I'll put them in our room where Bel can see them." She carried the vase carefully upstairs and stood for a while in the middle of the bedroom trying to decide where to put it. The desk, she thought, that's the best place. She'll see it much better if it's there. Josie pottered around the room for a few moments, unsure what to do next. I wish Bel would come home. I wish it was tomorrow. I wish Mum and Dad would come home. She lay down on her bed and closed her eyes and then opened them again at once because she was sure, suddenly, as sure as she had ever been of anything in her life before, that she was not alone in the room any longer. She sat up quickly and looked around. Nothing. No one. But the mirror . . . In one swift movement she was standing in front of the large round modern mirror in the blue plastic frame that was hanging on the wall on the other side of the bedroom. She peered into it. Nothing. Nothing at all, and yet, the feeling that she was not alone grew and grew so that she whirled around to look behind her again. And when she turned to face the mirror once more, there she was, Claire Daley. The image of her dark, laughing face was as thin as smoke, a veil across the mirror, no more, but she was there . . . she was coming back. Even as she looked, the lines of the face were growing less faint, her mouth was becoming firmer. Soon, soon she would see the teeth, and the black eyes and Bel would be home and this thing would begin to batten on her all over again. Josie felt no fear. There was no time for that. Hatred filled her.

Much later, weeping uncontrollably, she would say over and over again to her mother that she didn't remember anything. But that wasn't quite true. There was one thing she was quite, quite certain of.

"We could hear your shrieks halfway down the road," said her mother. "I really thought someone was murdering you. Shrieking and screaming. I've never in my life heard anything like it. Then we rushed up here at once and found you lying on the bed and that mirror turned into powder on the carpet. You'd ground it into dust. I think I'll have to change the carpet you know. I mean, why, darling? Whatever got into you? It's simply not like you. You're normally so sensible. Can you remember what made you do such a thing?"

Josie shook her head. Pretended ignorance. Her mother sighed.

"Those sounds. I'll never forget them. They didn't sound like you a bit."

Because they weren't, Josie thought, and smiled. That was the one thing she was sure of. She, Josie, had not uttered one sound while grinding the mirror into dust with the heels of her shoes. Not one sound. But she, too, had heard the screams, and knew whose screams they were, and she had stamped and stamped on every tiny shred of glass until there was nothing left of the mirror, until the screaming faded to a whisper, then to a silence like the silence of death itself.

6 The Doll Maker

Everyone who lived on the Burton Bridge estate knew Avril Clay. The children called her Auntie Avril. She was a small, unremarkable woman, given to wearing unsuitable hats (ruched velvet or massed flower petals) in all weathers. She lived in a neat little semi-detached house on Elmford Lane and her garden was full of tiny stone statues in unexpected places: not gnomes, but squirrels, birds, hedgehogs and even a stone deer. How she fits them into that pocket handkerchief of a garden, her neighbours used to say, we'll never know. She loved children. She said so herself. "Oh, I do love the kiddies, bless their hearts!" she would exclaim whenever she saw them playing on the swings in the park, or walking to school. The women shook their heads over the coffee cups and whispered:

"Such a shame that she never married and had children of her own. Ever so fond of them, she is. Such a pity."

It was a pity. No one knew it, no one suspected it because, after all, you don't go blurting these things out to everyone, but being childless meant, for Avril Clay, walking around with a raw wound hurting somewhere where no one could see it. A constant pain, a twisting and burning and aching that bit into the very corners of her soul.

"She's so good with her hands." That was another thing they said about her, and it was true. Every jumble sale, school fête, Christmas bazaar or bring-and-buy for miles around would be filled with the things she had made: jam and chutney and lavender bags and quilts for dolls and pyjama cases in the shape of bunny rabbits – there seemed to be nothing she couldn't turn her hand to.

"Miss Clay," the vicar used to say when confronted with her offerings, "that's a real labour of love."

On the first and third Wednesday of every month, Avril held a doll's surgery in her home. Girls sat in her front parlour, clutching their broken darlings, and one by one they would be called into the work-room at the back of the house (in turn, just like a proper doctor's surgery) and Auntie Avril wearing a flowered nylon overall, would look and diagnose and prescribe and place the dismembered creature on a shelf full of others like it.

"She'll be ready next week, dear," she'd say, "good as new. Don't worry your little head about it any more. Will you send the next person in as you leave, please? Thank you."

Ruth went into the workroom and looked down at the floor.

"Hello, Ruth dear," said Avril. "Come and sit

down and show me what's the matter. Don't be shy."

Ruth sat down.

"Have a dolly mixture, love," Avril continued. "Dolly mixtures for doll's surgery. I think that's appropriate, don't you?" She laughed, and Ruth gave a timid half-smile.

"Her head's come off," she said, "and I can't seem to get it on."

"Let's have a look." Avril took the doll. "Oh, what a beauty she is, isn't she? Aren't you lucky? Eh? Such a lucky girl. Hasn't she got lovely hair, though? I don't think I've seen such hair for ages. Marvellous, like a forest in autumn." Avril stroked the hair with greedy fingers. "She'll be ready next week, dear. You can call in any day after Tuesday. I'm always in in the afternoon."

"Thank you very much, Auntie Avril." Ruth stood up to go, and then blushed. "Please may I go to the toilet?"

"Yes, of course, dear. First on the right at the top of the stairs. Will you send my next customer in on your way?"

"Yes, of course. And thank you."

Ruth waited until the door had shut behind Sandra and then went upstairs. She had no intention of going anywhere near the toilet. That was an excuse. She was going to look at the Room. They all called it that, everyone she knew who had been to Auntie Avril's. Angela was the only one who had ever seen inside it. She had told Ruth:

"It's upstairs next to the loo. You should have a look in there. It's really . . . I don't know . . . peculiar."

"What's in there?" Ruth had asked.

"Only dolls and things. Nothing scary, but I don't know . . . it gave me the creeps."

Ruth opened the door. It was a very small room, only a boxroom, really. There was a table pushed up against the window. On the walls there were hooks: hundreds of them, and hanging from the hooks were arms and legs and even bald doll's heads with empty eye sockets, dangling in such a way as to make them seem alive, like bits of very small children. There was a shelf stacked with limbless bodies, plastic torsos waiting. Waiting to be made whole. Another shelf had small wigs balanced on rows and rows of little sticks. A large biscuit tin lay open on the table, and Ruth went to look into it and drew back quickly. That's horrible, she thought, and then: how silly I am. It's only eyes . . . bits of plastic and glass, that's all. But the way they stared up at her, hard and unblinking and the way they just seemed about to roll around, or move, and all their different colours . . . She left the room and closed the door behind her.

Later, she said to Angela:

"I went up there. To the Room. I didn't think it was so bad. The eyes were a bit creepy. But it's only bits of dolls, after all. She couldn't mend our dolls if she didn't have any spare parts, could she?"

Angela said: "I suppose not. But all those legs and arms and things, just hanging there. I was in there for quite a long time. I tell you, after a bit they begin to look human in a funny kind of way. Especially the hands. Everything seemed . . . I can't describe it . . . as if it was going to move the minute I left, or as if it had just stopped moving when I went in."

"Are you going to come with me when I collect Meg?"

"O.K." said Angela. "When are you going?"

"Thursday. Jackie and Sandra are going then too."

"Then we can all go straight from school. What's wrong with Jackie's doll? I know Sandra's brother broke the arms off her Alice."

"Jackie's doll had her legs squashed. Both smashed to pieces. Someone dumped a chest-of-drawers down on top of her when they were moving."

"Is that Elaine? That doll with the marvellous eyes? The one she got from America?"

"Yes," said Ruth. "I've never see a doll with eyes like that. Kind of halfway between blue and mauve."

"The thing about them is, they look real. Not like doll's eyes at all. I wish I could get one like that."

"Fat chance, round here."

Avril was working. Remove. Replace. Sort. Cut. Glue. She was humming to herself. Somewhere, deep inside where the Pain always was, she felt small stirrings of joy, of anticipation, of pleasure, such as she imagined a woman must feel when she was aware, for the first time, of a living child growing within her. Avril worked late. Choose. Change. Mould and twist. Make and yearn. All through the night.

Ruth's mother said: "I see Auntie Avril mended Meg for you. That's good."

"Yes, I suppose so," Ruth sighed.

"What do you mean, you suppose so? You know how fond you are of that doll. Aren't you pleased to have her back in one piece?"

"Yes, I am. Of course I am. But she's different . . ."

"No, she's not. She looks exactly the same to me."

Ruth shook her head. "She's not the same. Her hair's not the same."

"What's the matter with it?"

"It used to be silky," said Ruth. "Don't you remember? And that lovely colour, like chestnuts, and now it's all nylonish and stiff and just an ordinary brown."

"Let's have a look." Ruth's mother looked closely at the doll's head. "It seems exactly the same to me, I promise you."

"It's not. I know it's not."

"But it must be. Auntie Avril wouldn't have needed to touch the hair. She was only supposed to be fixing the head into place. Why would she touch the hair?"

"She didn't need to touch the hair at all. But she has."

"Why, though?"

"I don't know why. I just know that this hair is awful. I think she stole Meg's hair, that's what."

"Oh, don't be so silly, Ruth. Whatever would she want to do a thing like that for? It's very naughty to say such things about anyone, let alone poor old Avril. Don't let me hear you say that again. Stealing indeed!"

Ruth didn't answer. She went upstairs and sat on her bed and looked at Meg. If Auntie Avril *had* stolen Meg's hair, where was it now? On that shelf in the boxroom? Why? Why had Auntie Avril done it? Ruth shivered.

Jackie and Sandra were playing in Jackie's bedroom. Jackie said:

"You know Ruth's doll, Meg? Well, I saw her the other day and her hair is different. Meg's hair, and you say Alice's skin is all funny, and just look at Elaine's eyes."

Elaine, of the famous lilac-coloured eyes, all the way from America, was lying on the floor. Sandra picked her up. Her eyes were a flat, dull blue.

"Gosh," Sandra said, "they *are* different. I can see it quite clearly. We were all dead jealous of your Elaine's eyes. Did you tell your mother?"

"Yes, and my dad. They thought I was crazy. Swore blind that the eyes were the same as they always were. Said I had too much imagination, and anyway . . ." Jackie paused.

"What?"

"They said that as it was the legs of my doll that were broken, they were the bits that would have been replaced. She'd not have needed to go near the eyes, would she?"

"No, she wouldn't. But she did, didn't she?"

"Yes."

"But why?"

"I don't know. Your Alice only needed her arms fixed and now you say her skin is all funny. Actually . . ."

"What?"

"I don't see how she could fiddle with a doll's skin, do you? I mean, she couldn't just peel it off, could she?"

"I know you don't believe me," Sandra said, "but it's true. I don't know how she did it. Or what for. But Alice had a special skin. A special sort of colour. I always thought she looked more . . . alive, more real, because of it. It had a kind of glow to it as if . . ." Sandra broke off, unable to find the right words. Then she said: "As if she were a real person. It even felt softer than a doll's skin normally does."

"Did you tell your parents?"

"No."

"Why not?"

"They wouldn't believe me. I don't even think you and Ruth and Angela believe me."

"I do," said Jackie. "At least, I think I do. But what can we do about it? We can't go back to Auntie Avril and complain, can we?"

"No," Sandra shook her head.

"Then what can we do?"

"Forget about it, I suppose. But I do think it's odd, all the same."

A notice went up outside Avril Clay's house in Elmford Lane. It said: 'There will be no dolls' surgeries for the next two months, because of family problems'.

The children told their mothers, who speculated over the coffee cups. What problems? If it came right down to it, what family? Wasn't there a sister in Canada? No, not a sister. A cousin, that's right. But in Canada. Had anyone seen Avril lately? And why had she missed the Farlow Road High School Fête for the first time in years? Should we call round and see if she's all right? She may be ill. But somehow, no one felt they knew her well enough to intrude, and anyway she couldn't be ill, because Mrs. Webb had seen her at the shops and Jane and Sally had waved to her the other day in the park, they'd said, and she was very cheery. Her hat was covered in pink blossoms, apparently. That doesn't sound like someone who's sick, now does it? All the same . . .

Avril worked at night, behind drawn curtains. Every night. It was the hardest, most delicate work she had ever done. In her heart, the years of wanting and hurting and longing were like a machine powering her fingers, driving her skilful hands. She never stopped. Choose. Cut. Sew. Make. Bind. Mould. And, at last, behind drawn curtains, it was finished. A labour of love indeed. A labour of more than love.

The dolls' surgery reopened. There was no more speculation. Avril told everyone she met that Hazel, her cousin's child, was coming to live with her. The cousin, poor woman, had died, far away in Canada and who could the poor child live with but Avril?

"I'm very sorry for my cousin, of course," she would say to anyone who would listen. "Losing her husband, and now this . . . but I'll be so happy to have Hazel. It'll be just like having a child of my own. And you know how I love the kiddies!"

The women nodded, and talked of blessings in disguise, and ill winds blowing no good, and Hazel's loss being Avril's gain.

Ruth and Jackie and Sandra spread the word among their friends. Those girls who took their dolls to the surgery and sneaked upstairs to look into the room, reported that it was always locked. No way of finding out what had happened to Meg's hair and Elaine's eyes. As for Alice's skin, well, most of the girls concluded that Sandra had only made that up so as not to be left out. Sandra, however, knew she hadn't, and sometimes at night, she dreamed of Auntie Avril, peeling away the layers of Alice's soft skin with her bare hands.

"That's Hazel, look. Over there." Ruth pointed.

"Where?" Jackie craned her neck to see.

"I can see her," said Angela.

"She's awfully pretty," Sandra added. "Let's go over and talk to her."

"She's only a first year, though," said Ruth. "Won't she think it's a bit peculiar if we all come up to her at once?"

"Well, we don't have to talk to her, do we?" said Jackie. "Just go a little closer. Have a look. She looks ever so nice."

"Yes, lovely," said Sandra. "I'm going."

They walked over to the bench on which Hazel was sitting with her new friends. Ruth stared at her, fascinated. Her hair, in the September sunshine shone like chestnuts, all the colours of the leaves in autumn. Her skin glowed as if it were lit from within. Sandra thought: Alice's skin was just like that. I wish I could touch it and see. Hazel looked up.

Jackie gasped and ran away. Ruth and Sandra ran after her.

"Whatever's wrong, Jackie? What's the matter?"

"Her eyes! Did you see them? Did you?"

"No, what was wrong with them?" said Angela.

"They're Elaine's eyes. That's what. She's got eyes like Elaine. Exactly the same."

"It's a coincidence, that's all," said Ruth.

"I don't believe it!" Jackie was shouting. "I just don't believe it. Look at her! Look at her hair and her skin! I think Auntie Avril stole bits from all our dolls, and probably from others as well, and made herself a person, that's what I think!"

"You're crazy."

"That's impossible . . ."

"You'd better not go round saying that," said Angela quietly, "or people will think you're mad. Even if it's true. Especially if it's true. They will take you away if you say things like that. Really. Don't say it any more."

And so the girls said nothing. But they knew. They never played with Hazel. If she came to the playground in the park, they left quickly and went to feed the ducks instead.

7 The Graveyard Girl

I'm Teresa Wignall. I remember. I do remember that, though I've forgotten other things. I remember pieces of my life, but they're fading. There's a face looking worried, which is my mother's face, I think, but I can't call it to mind properly any more. There are children. They'd be my brothers and sisters, I suppose, but their names are gone and what they looked like, too. Sometimes, I'll see a child and the beginnings of a memory will stir in me like a dead leaf blowing, but it's gone. It's all gone. I drift about here and watch the seasons turning. There are roses in the summer and leaves in autumn to cover the graves and pile into small hills along the paths. And behind the wall, there is the school. The seasons turn and I watch. All the children. They come in the morning. If the windows are open, I can hear them singing. I can see them jumping in the playground, skipping, chanting rhymes:

> Here comes the doctor,
> Here comes the nurse,
> Here comes the lady
> With the alligator purse . . .

The children make the windows pretty. In winter, they stick paper snowflakes all over them. Lambs and flowers in the spring. Orange and yellow and red leaves in the autumn and then it's winter again. Round and round they go, the seasons. The children come and go. Sometimes, they are gone for weeks and then they come back again. They come back, and grow and learn and play and talk. I sit on the wall and watch them. I lean over the wall and listen to stories floating out of the windows. I wish I could be like them. I remember stories from before. At Sunday School there was a lady with a long dress and a hat trimmed with fur who read to us from a big book. I sit on the wall and wait. Sometimes, one of the children looks in my direction, but they don't see me. I have waited so long. Soon, soon I will be ready. I will be brave enough. I will go. I will. Go.

George Macmahon has been the caretaker of St. Peter's School for many years. He is a man devoted to shiny brass, shiny linoleum and shiny paintwork. He is the enemy of litter, dust, dirt and scratches on the tops of desks. He sweeps the playground every evening. There are always leaves blown across from the churchyard beyond the school wall, not to mention all the stuff the kids leave lying around during term time, and drifts of yellow bus tickets that blow in from the main road. George Macmahon is not a religious man, but he likes St. Peter's church next door. A no-nonsense building: tall with a high, square tower and a clock that you can rely on. No noisy chimes to interrupt your train of thought. The graveyard is a credit to Mr. Wiles, the gardener and handyman. No one's been buried there now for years and years. The corpses seem to go down to the huge Municipal Cemetery now, but the old graves in St. Peter's, with their blackened stones and chipped urns and mossy angels, are all kept as tidy as possible. All the grass is shaved as close as you please and tasteful roses, and discreet bushes of hydrangea, forsythia and suchlike, have been planted to cheer the place up a bit.

Mrs. Macmahon, who used to do school dinners in the old days but can't any more, on account of her bad legs, is of the opinion that it's asking for trouble, putting a school playground right beside a graveyard. Morbid, that's what she thinks it is, and anyway, some of those kids, you never know what they'll get up to. As for Mr. Macmahon, if he's told her once, he's told her a thousand times: "Never take any notice of it, that I've seen. Never. Been past it so often that they've stopped seeing it. Part of the furniture, that's all." Mrs. Macmahon shakes her head, purses her lips and pours herself another cup of tea. Sometimes she speaks and sometimes she doesn't bother and just thinks to herself: "Nevertheless. Them's dead people in there. Them's graves. Doesn't matter how old they are. Graves and kids together shouldn't be allowed. There might be ghosts."

Mrs. Macmahon also believes that ghosts are more likely to be found in old, disused graveyards. You can imagine a ghost coming to haunt you from a hundred years back or thereabouts, but to think of poor Ada Partridge, taken a month ago with pneumonia, flitting around like a blessed bit of fog – well, that was ridiculous. Mrs. Macmahon wouldn't, couldn't credit it. Ada a ghost! The thought made her giggle.

George Macmahon does not believe in ghosts at all. He's very firm on the subject. He says: "I should know, shouldn't I? Worked next door to gravestones all my life and never a glimmer of anything strange. Nothing." He tells anyone who'll listen. "You'll see people pass through of course. Only natural from time to time ... walking about. That's ordinary mortals. Nothing," as he puts it privately, "to get into a lather about. People, same as you and me."

The first day of term. The first day of a new school year. Mrs. Pike, in charge of Junior Two, is wearing a fluffy new cardigan with pearl buttons. The school smells clean. Clean rolled-up socks in all the pump-bags. Nice fresh painting overalls smelling of washing powder. No pictures are up yet in the corridors, after the summer holidays. The children are good. Still quiet. Excited. There are piles of new exercise books to be given out. Extra sharp pencils. Empty lockers, not a single sweet paper lurking. No crisp bags blowing about in the playground. Not yet.

Mrs. Pike says: "Good morning, Junior Two. Sit down in your places, please and let's see who we are. Hello, Susan dear. And Kevin. Well," she smiles, "there are lots of faces here I know already."

"Please, Miss," Wendy's hand waves in the air. "Please, Miss."

"Quiet, everyone," Mrs. Pike says firmly. "What is it, dear?"

"Please, Miss, there's a new girl. She's called Teresa."

"Thank you, dear. Now let us all sit down and I shall take the register and then we shall see who is and who isn't here."

The children are quiet. The rocking, up-and-down chanting of names, the repeated 'Yes Miss' thirty times over, settles over the room like a lullaby. Mrs. Pike closes the register.

"Please, Miss," says Wendy. "You haven't said Teresa."

"Well, Teresa," says Mrs. Pike, "stand up, dear, and let's look at you."

A very thin, small child with long, pale hair stands up at the back of the room. Mrs. Pike thinks: whatever will they send them wearing next? Fancy such a long and fussy dress for school. And none too clean by the looks of it. She says:

"What is your name, dear?"

"Teresa Wignall."

"How old are you?"

"I'm nine."

"And are you new?"

"Yes, Miss."

"Have you moved from another school?"

A pause. The child hestitates. Then:

"I've only just come . . ."

"Oh, I see. You're new to the area, are you, dear? Have you just moved here?"

"Yes, Miss."

Mrs. Pike sighs. She thinks: why does nobody tell me anything? Here is a completely new child and I haven't had any particulars, no address, no phone number. Nothing. And fine parents she must have, not even coming in with their child on the very first day at a new school. Mrs. Pike has views about parents. Some parents at any rate. She says, quite kindly, "Could I have your address, please."

The child bites her lip and looks desperately round the classroom. She looks almost as though she has forgotten, but "24 Anscoat Avenue," she says at last.

"Anscoat Avenue," Mrs. Pike repeats. "I'm afraid I don't know it. Are you sure it's not your old address? Where you used to live?"

"Yes, Miss."

"Is it quite near?"

"Yes, Miss."

"And will you be staying for dinner or going home?"

"I don't know, Miss."

"Well, have you brought dinner money?"

"No, Miss."

"Then perhaps you'd better go home, just for today and see what your mother says." Mrs. Pike smiles. Why is the child looking so terrified? Perhaps she's frightened of going home? Mrs. Pike adds: "Or you could stay, if you like, just for today. It may be a little far for you to go on your own. We'll sort out the money another day. Right, Teresa, go back to your desk. Wendy, will you and Susan look after Teresa today please, and see that she knows what to do, and where to go?"

"Will you read, Teresa, please, from the top of page five?"

Teresa bends her head. She has tears in her eyes. She whispers to Wendy: "I can't. I don't know how . . ."

"Shh. I'll help you. Listen to me." Wendy is a good reader. She mutters the words under her breath and Teresa repeats them slowly. Her voice falters.

"Please, Miss!" Nick puts his hand up.

"Yes, Nick?" Mrs. Pike frowns at him.

"Please, Miss, Wendy was helping her. I heard. She was telling her the words."

"That's no concern of yours, Nick," says Mrs. Pike calmly. "Carry on reading from where Teresa left off, please."

Mrs. Pike looks at Teresa while Nick is reading. She sits quite upright in her desk. The sunlight shines through the skin of her hands so that she seems almost transparent. I shall have to see what school she came from, Mrs. Pike thinks. Not a very good one, that's certain. She looks intelligent enough, but it's clear she can't read. As Nick sits down, Mrs. Pike puts R.R. next to Teresa's name on the register. Remedial Reading.

Nobody in Junior Two takes much notice of Samantha. She is quiet, ordinary-looking, not specially clever nor specially stupid. She is sitting in the desk beside Teresa Wignall, thinking, wondering whether or not she is feeling quite well. She feels cold. She didn't feel like that before she sat down. Walking over to the book corner to fetch a book was like stepping into a warm bath. Almost as soon as she left her desk she felt all right again, but the cold air washed over her as she sat down.

"Are you cold? Can you feel a draught?" she asks her neighbour, Mary.

"No, not really." Mary isn't interested.

Samantha feels dizzy, mad, peculiar, but she

is sure the cold is coming from Teresa. How can that be? She turns to look at the new girl, sitting silently with her hands folded in her lap. Impulsively, she puts a hand out as if to touch her, then draws it back, frightened. The air around Teresa is burning cold. Touching it is like laying fingers on a block of solid ice.

At playtime, Wendy pulls Nick's hair for telling tales. Nick kicks Wendy and the teacher on duty in the playground sends them to stand outside the staffroom door until lessons begin.

Wendy says: "Sh, they're talking about Teresa in there. Let's listen."

"Who cares about stupid old Teresa?" Nick is sulky. It's not his idea of playtime, milling about outside the staffroom door. Wendy comes close to the door to listen. The Headmaster has a carrying voice. Bits of what he's saying creep through to Wendy and she puts them together, like a jigsaw.

"Never heard of her . . . no new children in Junior Two that I know of . . . Wignall . . . Anscoat Avenue . . . I don't know . . . write to the Education Authority of course . . . got to have come from somewhere . . . there'd be a record if she's just moved here from another part of the country . . . Anscoat Avenue, isn't that one of the little streets behind the White Lion? . . . Rings a bell . . . Remedial Reading, you say? . . . Better give her Free Dinners till we find out more about her ... sounds like a case of neglect ... I don't know ... I honestly don't know how parents expect us to do the lot single-handed."

Samantha watches Teresa as the children form a line to walk to the canteen. The cold feeling has gone. Perhaps, thinks Samantha, it is because we're outside, but now there is a mistiness around Teresa's head.

"Can you see a kind of mist around Teresa's head?" Samantha asks Julie.

"You need your eyes looking at," says Julie and turns to talk to someone else.

Maybe I do, Samantha thinks. Maybe the mist is in my eyes. But she knows it isn't.

Afternoon playtime. Teresa is standing with Wendy and Susan in a patch of sunlight by the graveyard wall.

"I like your dress," Wendy says. "I wish my mum would let me wear my long dress to school."

"I would like a dress like yours," Teresa says. She speaks so quietly that the others have to bend their heads to hear her.

"I would like ..." she begins, then shakes her head.

"What?" Susan says.

"My mother is dead," Teresa says suddenly. Wendy is the first to speak, after the silence.

"Who do you live with, then? Your father? Have you got any brothers or sisters?"

"No," Teresa shakes her head. "Not any more."

The girls are going to ask more questions, but the bell goes. The next lesson is P.E.

Mrs. Pike comes prepared. She has found an old leotard in the Lost Property cupboard, and some shabby pumps. She tries to hand them to Teresa discreetly, so as not to embarrass the child, but everyone notices and a whisper goes round the cloakroom:

"Teresa Wignall's not got any P.E. things of her own."

"Must be dead poor."

"Bit weird, if you ask me."

"It's not her fault. She can't help it."

"Must be daft, not bringing P.E. stuff."

A surprise! Teresa can float over the highest boxes with no effort at all. She can balance on the narrowest bar of all, she seems almost to be weightless. Mrs. Pike is delighted and lavish with her praise. Even the boys are silenced. By the end of the lesson, Nick has put forward a theory that Teresa is a runaway from a travelling circus. Well, it would fit the facts, wouldn't it? Funny clothes, no money, can't read . . . it fits. It does.

Samantha's mother is always one of the last to

get to the playground. Samantha has often asked to go home by herself, or with a friend, and the answer is always the same: "When you're ten, dear." So Samantha waits by the railings quite patiently. She likes looking at everyone else's mums. There's Teresa, she thinks, but where's her mother? There are no grown-ups anywhere near her. Perhaps she's allowed to walk home alone . . . lucky thing. Samantha watches her walking out of the gate. The mistiness is still clinging to her outline. Then she's gone. Samantha waits and then becomes aware of someone watching her from the churchyard. She turns and is just in time to see a flash of pale hair ducking down behind the wall. Silly, she thinks, it could be anyone. But she knows it isn't. She knows who it is. Teresa. There's something very strange about Teresa. Samantha is frightened of her. But, she thinks, I wish I knew what I was frightened of. Exactly what it was.

Wendy and Susan walk home together. Wendy's mum fetches them both.

"Did you see where Teresa went?" says Susan.

"No, I didn't. One minute she was there in the cloakroom and the next minute she was gone."

"Must look tomorrow. I want to see if anyone fetches her. Probably one of the Orphanage people." Susan looks knowing. She and Wendy and Liz have decided that Teresa lives in an orphanage. Nick's circus theory is O.K. but, as

Liz puts it, "She's got to live somewhere now, hasn't she? Even if she has run away."

From:
Headmaster
St. Peter's School
Wallington
5 September 1983

To: Chief Education Officer
Sceptre House
Wordsworth Crescent

Dear Sir
I am writing to ask whether you have any record of a Teresa Wignall, aged 9, of 24 Anscoat Avenue, Wallington. She has arrived in my school with no documentation whatsoever and I would be grateful for any particulars that you can give me about her previous background.

Yours faithfully,
Frank Swithin.

Tomorrow. Tomorrow I will have to tell them. I will tell Wendy and Susan. They will be frightened. Will they still talk to me? But I must tell them. Otherwise they will ask and ask, question after question and I shan't be able to answer. I am going to learn to read. All by myself with Miss Harris. I can tell the letters. I can remember them, after all this time. I can make them with a pencil. And I can read some words. Soon I will be able to read whole stories. I know the numbers. I can add them together a little. I will learn so much. And they will help me to learn. Not Mrs. Pike. Mrs. Pike wouldn't believe me. Wouldn't believe in me. And then how could I stay?

Wendy, Susan and Teresa are sitting in a corner of the cloakroom, half-hidden by coats. The others have gone out to play. Susan is crying quietly. She has shrunk away a little from Teresa and Wendy. Wendy is trembling all over, but she manages to speak.

"If you are . . . what you say you are, then prove it. Or we won't believe you. Go on. Prove it. Go through that wall. Then we'll know you're not fibbing."

"Are you sure you want me to?" Teresa whispers.

"Yes."

"And you, Susan?"

"Stop snivelling, Susan, or she'll never show us," Wendy says.

Teresa walks over to the wall and disappears.

Then she slides out from between the basins, seeping out of the wall like a transparent formless mist that gradually takes on Teresa's shape and then thickens, becomes a person.

"It's like colouring in a drawing!" Susan

squeals. "At first you were just an outline and then you sort of filled yourself in. Please do it again."

Teresa shakes her head. "No, I daren't. I want . . . I want to be like you. I would like you to be my friends. Will you tell the others? They'll be frightened. You were frightened at first. But please don't tell anyone else . . . in another class, or in your families . . . Please."

"O.K." says Wendy. "We won't, will we?" She glares round at Susan.

"Of course we won't, silly. But will you tell us things?" Susan wants to know. "Like what it's like to be a ghost? Do you sleep and eat and that? Do you talk to other ghosts? Do you haunt people? Will you tell us, Teresa, please?"

"It's long," Teresa says. "It's long and weary. You watch the seasons turning and know that it's forever. It's very long . . . I've seen so many children from over the wall. It's a long time till you have the courage to join in. I hear the songs and the stories from the other side of the wall. I want to learn. I want to play. That's all."

The bell goes. Junior Two bustle into the classroom. Wendy and Susan link arms with Teresa. They carry Teresa's secret clutched tight within them: something precious, something rare. Time enough to tell the others later on.

From: Chief Education Officer
Sceptre House
Wordsworth Crescent
12 September 1983

To: Frank Swithin, M.A.
St. Peter's School
Wallington

Dear Sir

With reference to your letter about Teresa
Wignall, I have to inform you that I am unable
to find a record of this child. I am, however,
making further enquiries, and will let you know
as soon as I have any information at all.

Yours faithfully,
Horace Underhill.

Frank Swithin, Headmaster, snorts loudly. The
tip of his nose has turned purple – a sign of
rage.

"Bloody incompetents at Sceptre House!" he
bellows. "Not a blind bit of use at all." He sighs,
shakes his head and coughs. The tip of his nose
subsides to a pale shade of mauve. He mutters to
Mrs. Pike:

"Never mind, dear Mrs. Pike. I'm sure you're
doing a grand job. Any child that turns up in this
school is to be taught. Am I right? Or am I
wrong?"

"Absolutely right, Mr. Swithin," Mrs. Pike says quietly. "Absolutely."

"Good, good," says Mr. Swithin. The tip of his nose is pink once more. Quite normal.

The days go by. Junior Two is a class with a ghost in it. The children have become accustomed to the thought. At first, of course, it was different. Samantha fainted when she heard. Julie had hysterics and had to be taken home. Nick and Kevin wanted to tell everyone: newspapers, teachers, television, the whole world, but Wendy had told them what would happen if they did: they would be haunted all their lives by the very horriblest ghosts in the universe. Teresa had said so, Wendy whispered. It wasn't true. Teresa had said nothing of the kind, but it worked. Nick and Kevin were silent. Dinners were a problem at first, because Teresa could not eat, but all the children helped. One speared up the meat and ate it while the dinner lady's back was turned, another slid the vegetables off Teresa's plate, and Samantha (who ate everything that other people hated, like rice pudding and sago and stewed gooseberries and lumpy custard) generally dealt with the afters.

One day each member of the class was given a small envelope and told to collect as much money as they could for the blind.

"We'll each bring two pence extra," Susan had announced, "and put it in Teresa's envelope."

At the end of the week, Teresa had fifty-eight pence and Mrs. Pike was very pleased. She hadn't expected half that sum.

"What a lot of money, dear," she said. "Well done."

"My friends helped me," Teresa said.

"That's what friends are for, aren't they, dear? And it's such a good cause."

The days go by. Junior Two is a class with a ghost in it. The children don't mind at all.

A class with a ghost in it. Sometimes, at playtime, Mrs. Pike's children congregate beside the bicycle shed to watch Teresa disappear through the wall and reappear again. Three children keep watch, make sure that no one is looking. Nick asks Teresa to float right over the wall: up and over like a bird, and Teresa does so. Everyone claps. Teresa enjoys the applause, the admiration, being someone special . . .

A class with a ghost in it. The children are making little linen mats, embroidering them with coloured silks. Teresa threads the needle right through her hand, as though it weren't there at all, and feels nothing. Wendy and Liz think this is very impressive.

"Do it again," they whisper.

"No, don't," says Susan. "It's horrid. It makes me feel sick to look."

"Then don't look," says Wendy. "Turn your back to us. Baby!"

Teresa does it again, just to oblige her friends.

A class with a ghost in it. Mrs. Pike calls Teresa to her desk.

"How are you getting on, dear? I hear good things about you from Miss Harris. She says you're reading very well now. Are you enjoying school?"

"Oh, yes, Miss." Teresa nods vigorously.

"There's just one thing," Mrs. Pike frowns. "I would like to see your mother, dear. Do you think you could ask her to come and see me one day?" Mrs. Pike is thinking: How can anyone let their child wear the same clothes, day in, day out? Mrs. Pike refuses to believe that anyone can be so poor or so neglectful. Teresa hangs her head. Mrs. Pike persists.

"Will you, dear? Will you ask her to come and see me? I'd like to meet her. And I'd like to tell her how well you're getting on."

"She can't come," Teresa says suddenly. "She's ill. In hospital."

Mrs. Pike says: "Oh dear. Poor thing. Will she be there long? Who is looking after you? Is it your father? Perhaps he could come?"

"He's dead."

"Oh, goodness, I am sorry," Mrs. Pike is confused. This is a matter for the Head. But . . .

"You must be looked after by somebody . . ."

"My auntie," says Teresa after a pause. "But she couldn't come in. She's ever so busy. She's

123

got a new baby. I don't think she'll come in."

"Very well, dear," Mrs. Pike sighs. "Go back and finish your sums."

She thinks to herself: this is a case for the Social Security if ever I saw one. I shall go round there tomorrow night and speak to the aunt. It shouldn't be allowed, such a nice little girl, so quiet and such a hard worker – and the children all seem to like her and be protective of her. Mrs. Pike makes a note on her memo pad: look up Anscoat Avenue in the *A to Z*.

Two days later, Mrs. Pike and Mr. Swithin have a serious talk about Teresa.

"I went myself, in the end," says Mrs. Pike. "I found Anscoat Avenue. I found number 24. It's a Chinese takeaway. No one there had ever heard of Teresa Wignall. I tried number 42. And number 2. And 4. No one had heard of her." Poor Mrs. Pike is at a loss. Worried. "She must live somewhere. She's a truthful child, I'm sure. Why would she say Anscoat Avenue if that isn't where she lives?"

Mr. Swithin grunts. "I'll write to the Education office again. Chivvy them up a bit. Don't you worry about it, Mrs. Pike. You're doing a grand job with the child. She's coming on splendidly."

Junior Two is a class with a ghost in it. A ghost who is coming on splendidly.

Miss Harris feels pleased. This Teresa Wignall has made good progress. Learned such a lot. She reads well now. A little slowly, but well. It is a sunny afternoon in October. Outside, the air has some of the sharpness of autumn in it, but in the classroom you could imagine it was summer still. It's a Friday. The end of a long week. Teresa is reading aloud, but Miss Harris is tired. The warmth has made her drowsy. She is thinking of tonight. Tonight she will put on her red jersey dress and go out to dinner with her fiancé and they will talk. Teresa has a soft voice. It melts into the warmth of the classroom, almost lulling Miss Harris to sleep:

"The witch pushed Gretel up close to the oven. The fire was roaring and spitting, burning with flames that leapt and jumped out of the door, nearly scorching her dress. 'Look in, my dear,' said the witch, 'to see if it's properly heated, and then we'll bake the bread.'

'I don't know how to,' said Gretel. 'Will you show me, please?'

'It's easy,' said the witch. 'Look, I'll show you.' She stood by her side, and as she bent towards the flames, Gretel pushed her right in the fire, shut the iron door and locked her in with the flames . . ." Teresa's voice fades to nothing. roused suddenly by the silence. "We'll have to stop now, but you can keep the book for the weekend if you like." She gathers her papers together. Stands up.

"No, thank you, Miss," says Teresa. She is shaking, nearly in tears.

"It's a horrible book. I hate it."

"But it ends happily, dear. Really it does. That's the wicked witch you know, who was going to eat Hansel. She deserves it, doesn't she?"

"Nobody deserves it," Teresa whispers. "Nobody. Nobody deserves that."

Miss Harris sighs. "Perhaps you're right. It is rather gruesome. Never mind, we'll find a happy story next week."

Teresa slips from the room. Miss Harris is already thinking of what she will tell her fiancé: "Imagine it, Neil. A child in this day and age, with all that violence on television, who trembles at Hansel and Gretel. I've noticed, of course, that she is a sensitive child."

I remember now. That story reminded me. I remember fire. Paint bubbling on the window-sills, paper curling into long black rolls, the bannisters lit up with bars of shining white and yellow. And the smoke. Filling my mouth like water, filling my eyes and burning them and choking me, a fog everywhere. Everywhere. Nowhere that wasn't a fog, a sooty, smelly blanket over everything. The smell of things scorching. And sounds. Tearing and crashing and the roar of the flames, and over everything else, screaming. I remember it all now. I know how I died. But the others – did they die too? There's none of them buried here. I know that.

George Macmahon is sweeping leaves, marvelling as he does every year that such quantities of them should land in his playground from trees that don't look more than ordinarily leafy in the summer. The children, of course, make it worse, gathering them into heaps all over the place, spreading them into patterns, kicking them this way and that. He groans. Not long now. A few more weeks, then retirement. Most of the time, George thinks of the idle days that are coming with something like dread, but not on a bitter cold afternoon like this. He turns his mind, deliberately, to gas fires, slippers, hot tea, toast, television . . . nearly done now. On this way to the shed to put away the broom, he catches sight of someone in the graveyard. A child, wandering around.

"Here, you!" he calls. "Aren't you one of our kids?"

The child stops. Looks at him. Nods silently. George turns red with fury. Bloody kids! Never a thought for their parents, most likely worried sick. He shouts at the little girl:

"Get off home now! Go on. Your mam'll be that worried. Go on now, hurry up. The bell went twenty minutes ago. You'll catch your death out here."

The child runs away. George shakes his head. Whatever next? Parents to blame as much as the kids, when you stop to think. What kind of parent wouldn't come and meet a little thing like that on a dark afternoon? Asking for trouble, were some people. Asking for it.

From: Chief Education Officer
Sceptre House
Wordsworth Crescent
3 November 1983

To: Frank Swithin, M.A.
St. Peter's School
Wallington

Dear Sir

Further to your recent enquiry, I should like to assure you that we have in no way let the matter drop, as you put it. You are certainly aware of the time such things can take and the care with which we have to check all the facts that become available to us. We have been in touch with ten other Local Authorities in the immediate vicinity with no success. We have found six Teresa Wignalls but all six have been verified as attending other schools.

We could, of course, extend our search to cover the whole country, and will do so if necessary. However, certain facts have come to light which may be of interest to you.

1) 24 Anscoat Avenue is now a Chinese Takeaway shop with a flat above it. This flat is lived in by the proprietors of the afore-mentioned eating place.

2) We have traced the previous owners of the property through local Estate Agents. The house was rebuilt in 1903 after having been destroyed by fire in July of 1902. The householder at the time of the fire was a Mrs. Frances Wignall, a mother of five children. One child, Teresa Wignall, aged nine, died in the blaze. There is no further record of this family.

It is only as an interesting coincidence that I draw these facts to your attention. It is, of course, clearly impossible that a child who died some eighty years ago should be attending your school. You may rest assured therefore, that we shall be pursuing our enquiries.

Yours Sincerely
Horace Underhill.

Several members of staff feel distinctly faint when Mr. Swithin reads out the letter to a hastily assembled Staff Meeting at the end of the afternoon.

Teresa, hiding in the lavatories till everyone else had gone home, hears loud voices coming from the staff room, and listens. Mr. Swithin is shouting:

"It's all a lot of nonsense. A mistake. I don't believe in ghosts. Never have and never will, and the idea of having one in my school, mixing with our children is simply monstrous. I will not stand for it and that's that. Mrs. Pike, don't cry, please. You will tackle the child in the morning and that'll put an end, once and for all to this ghost rubbish. I've never heard anything like it in my life. There's many a funny letter I've had from the Education Authority in my time, but this beats all, it does really. A ghost in my school! How can rational adults even begin to believe such things?"

Teresa drifts out to the playground, over the wall, back to the graveyard. She looks at the dark windows of the school – her school – and wishes she could remember how to cry. She thinks: I can never go there again. Mr. Swithin doesn't want me there, mixing with the other children. I'm bad for them. He doesn't believe in me. I can't show myself again. They mustn't see me. They'll get into trouble. Monstrous, that's what he said. Monstrous. I shall see them and they'll never know. I must say goodbye, but how? How?

Junior Two is quiet today. Teresa, Mrs. Pike says, trying to look cheerful, will not be coming back. We will all miss her, she says, and there are tears in her eyes. Some of the children are crying.

"Open your reading books, children," says Mrs. Pike. Wendy opens her book and finds a small piece of paper tucked between the pages. 'Dear Wendy. They have found out about me. I can't come back because Mr. Swithin will be cross and not allow it. I will miss you. Please come to the wall and wave because I will be looking for you though you may not be able to see me any more now. Thank you for looking after me. Love to everyone. Teresa.'

Wendy bursts into noisy tears and doesn't stop crying till milktime.

Wendy, Susan, Liz, Nick and Kevin stand by the graveyard wall and wave.

"D'you think she's there?" Liz asks.

"'Course she is," says Wendy. "She said she would be, didn't she?"

She raises her voice: "Teresa! Hello! Can you see me?"

"Don't be daft, Wendy," says Nick. "Whatever do you think you look like, shouting into the air like that?"

"I'm going to shout," says Wendy, "so there. I don't want Teresa to think we've forgotten her."

Christmas comes, and then January. A new term. The children of Junior Two no longer stand and wave by the graveyard wall. The memory of Teresa begins to fade. Occasionally, Wendy will turn and shout over the wall, raise her hand, but even she does so less and less frequently. It's not that Junior Two have forgotten Teresa; only that she is no longer in the very top layer of their minds. Thoughts of her lie in corners of the memory, like dreams from the night before last.

Mr. Edgeburton is the new Caretaker. He is stiff and thin and quiet. He has bushy eyebrows. He never smiles. Once upon a time, he was in the Navy. Or the Army, no one knows for sure. He walks very upright, as though on parade. He is not given to gossiping with either the staff or the children. But he keeps the place spick and span, there's no denying it. He is keen on security. He has had locks made for every room in the school, and patrols the corridors every afternoon, locking up. One day, as he is about to turn the key in the Library door, he notices a child reading in the corner. He knows exactly how to deal with the situation. He strides into the room and towers over the small child. "Hello, hello, hello," he says, "what have we here, then? An eager scholar, is it? Come along now, girl, what time do you call this? Get along home this instant, before I lock you in here for the night."

The child looks at him. Stands up and puts the book back on the shelf. "I'm sorry," she whispers as she slides out of the door. "I should think so too! Whatever next? I've heard of playing truant from school, but I've never heard of a child who played truant from home." He almost smiles at his own joke, but the child has gone.

He locks the Library door, and carries on down the corridor, rattling his keys. Feeling important.

I will go back, Teresa thinks. I will go back after he has gone home, and finish the book. And then I will start another. There are friends in the books. People and children that are only half-real, like me. There is a world inside those pages that someone like me can live in for ever.

Mr. Edgeburton, having locked up, is on his way home. Turning back towards the school gates, he thinks he sees the half-transparent form of a girl float like a curl of smoke above the playground wall. He rubs his eyes and looks again. Nothing. All the way home, he worries about what it might have been. By the time he opens his front door, he has decided that it was only a sheet of newspaper, borne upwards by the wind.

8 The Light of Memory

Somebody, somewhere, had overlooked one side of Tibbet Street. The long row of tall houses, most of them nearly a hundred years old, seemed out of place standing opposite the blocks of flats known as Blenheim Court, embarrassed almost, their high windows veiled with dust, their hedges overgrown to hide the crumbling brickwork, shrinking back from the pavement behind small squares of untended grass.

"They should've done that side of the road at the same time as they did this side, shouldn't they?" Nick said. "It stands to reason."

Tony nodded and peered through a hole in one of the hedges.

"What're you doing?" asked Nick. "There's nothing to look at in there. The curtains are drawn."

"I'm only looking. That's all." Tony kicked a stone along the pavement.

"You were trying to play the Window Game, weren't you?"

"I was not."

"Were."

"Wasn't."

"Yes, you were." Nick started to run. "Well, you play it if you want. I'm going home. See you."

"See you," said Tony, and watched Nick disappear into the passage between two blocks of flats. Nick never played the Window Game any more. It's babyish, he'd said. It's boring. That's what he'd said, but Tony knew the real reason. He'd lost his nerve after that woman had complained to the coppers that these two little kids were always staring at her through the windows. Prowling about, she called it. Silly old bat. She'd only had to draw the curtains, after all, and then none of it would have happened. People were stupid, that was all. It wasn't illegal or anything to look, was it? There was no law, was there, that said you couldn't take a dekko into someone's front room? It was their silly fault if they sat there with all the lights on and the curtains open, Tony thought. It was almost as though they were asking to be looked at.

Tony had been playing the Window Game for years. It started when he used to come back from school with his mother. More often than not, she'd bump into some friend on the way and hang about in the street nattering and jabbering as if she'd forgotten he was there. He'd had to do something while he waited, so he looked into the houses, just to see what other people's front rooms were like. Sometimes he'd see someone in a room, and then he could think about who they were and what they were like and what they were going to have for tea. One house had had a fish tank in the front room. Tony could remember it quite clearly. All these fish swimming about in a glass box flooded with a greenish light, in and out of a plastic galleon about six inches long that was supposed to be a sunken treasure ship. He never saw anyone in that room with the fish and often wondered why a person would rig it all up and never even look at it.

He'd started coming home from school without his mother when he was seven.

"But only on condition that you come with Nick and come straight home," she'd said. Nick was eight and lived in the same flats, and Tony liked him so he didn't mind coming home with him. He'd shown Nick how to play the Window Game, and Nick really enjoyed it at first. In fact it was Nick's idea to come home along all kinds of different roads, because, he'd said: "You get fed up looking in the same windows all the time. I know some of these rooms as well as I know my own."

So they started walking down different streets. Some were better than others, of course. Waterloo Terrace was hopeless. Everyone had net curtains, which meant that you could see a bit but not enough. It was like looking at things through a fog. Marlborough Avenue was too posh. Everyone there seemed to whisk their heavy curtains across as soon as dusk fell, but sometimes Tony and Nick were lucky and someone forgot and the boys stood for minutes at a time staring in at the highly-polished furniture and the shelves full of books and, once or twice they even saw people. There was a party one evening in one of the houses, and everyone was milling about drinking out of tiny glasses and looking like actors on the television.

Nick *had* liked the Window Game, but, Tony thought, he was just a Nosy Parker. He liked seeing what he could, but then he'd just go home and forget about it. Not like me, Tony thought. Not like me at all. Tony never told Nick how he made things up, made stories up to go with what he'd seen. Invented people to live in the rooms if he hadn't managed to see who really lived there and, if he had glimpsed anyone, then he thought about who they were and what their names were and what they were going to say to one another. He devised whole lives for them. It made him feel good. He'd never told Nick and he could never have explained it to anyone, but it made him feel powerful, as if the houses on the way home from school were only doll's houses and as if his head were full of dolls like some toy box and he could open it up and take out his pretend people and put them in this room or that room and make them say or do exactly what he wanted.

But then there had been all that trouble with that Mrs. Bolsover, and Nick wasn't playing any more. He'd been scared off, and even Tony was having to be a bit more careful. He never stood and stared outside uncurtained windows any more, that was true, but he'd got so good at the Game that he could glance to the left or right as he walked down a street and take in enough. Enough to play the Game for a while, in his head. And anyway, he thought, if I don't see everything clearly it doesn't matter ... I can make it up. I can pretend about it, same as I can about the people, same as I can make up what they say.

The Hunchback of Notre Dame was standing at the bus stop. Tony crossed the road. He didn't have to cross the road just there. He could have walked on a bit, but the Hunchback filled him with a kind of terrified pity that made him want to turn and run whenever he caught sight of him and, at the same time, made him feel angry with himself for wanting to flee from this harmless old man. Nick had called him that: the Hunchback of Notre Dame. They'd seen the film on television. Actually, the Hunchback in the film, the real hunchback, looked a bit better, Nick had said. Calling him that, Nick said, was really quite flattering. Almost a compliment. And Tony had to admit it was true. The man was old. He was hunchbacked. He shuffled along in slippers most of the time. He wore a black, pinstriped suit that had moulded itself over the years to the shape of his body and glistened with age and dirt. But it was his face. His face was the worst part. His lower lip hung down almost to his chin. His nose spread and drifted across the middle of his face, his eyes wandered in their sockets like gooseberries in jelly, and then a hand, it seemed, had embedded its fingers in the flesh of his face and twisted it hard. Twisted it out of shape, like a child dissatisfied with something modelled out of plasticine. Tony shivered as he ran up the stairs. Poor old chap, he thought. It was easy to think that when the old geezer was safely out of sight. Tony could smell toast as he opened the door of the flat.

"Hi, Mum," he shouted. "What's for tea, then?"

The Hunchback of Notre Dame lay forgotten for the moment, deep in some corner of Tony's mind.

Tony couldn't sleep. He couldn't turn his light on and read because his mother would notice and then she'd be down on him like a ton of bricks. How're you going to get up for school tomorrow, growing boys need all the sleep they can get, etc, etc. Tony got out of bed, tiptoed across to his window and looked out. The big old houses on the other side of Tibbet Street had all been turned into flats ages ago. Lots and lots of windows for playing the Game with, but Tony had looked into them so often that he was bored with the lot of them. He hadn't even thought about them for months. Still, there was nothing else to do, was there? Most of them had the T.V. on over there. Blueish light shone out of a few. It wasn't healthy to watch television in the dark, but it saved on electricity, and a lot of people in those bed-sitters didn't have much money. Well, they wouldn't be living there if they had, Tony thought, with all the windows dirty and the paint peeling off the doors, and everyone saying the houses were going to be knocked down soon anyway. Tony didn't think that they would actually be demolished. People were always saying things like that.

He peered out of the window. What was that? In the corner house, the last one in the row, Number 16, someone had left one half of the curtain open. That's amazing, Tony thought. I've never seen that one open before. In the old days, Tony had grown frustrated with not getting a peep into that room, annoyed that the curtains were always closed, so he had furnished it in his own mind like a kind of witches' den, and made up a good, hermit-like witch to live in it, and left it at that. You never knew exactly who lived in all the different little flats, but Tony did know that Mrs. Richards lived in that particular house. He'd seen her often enough, going in through the gate pulling her shopping-trolley along behind her, so he'd cast her in the part of the Hermit-Witch. Poor old Mrs.

Richards, with her neat grey curls and her flat, purple felt hat! Tony laughed out loud. A less likely witch you never saw in your life. But she changed the minute she got into that darkened room, of course. Grew warts on her nose, and wore a sharp, pointed hat and had her broomstick propped up in the hall. In the umbrella stand.

Tony went on staring at the window. Number 16, first floor front. They had a funny kind of light on in there. Tony had never seen a light quite that colour before. It must have been a tinted bulb, but what colour? Pink? Gold? Orange? He couldn't tell, but it was a warm, blushing, creamy, yellow light, a light that warmed him as he looked at it, a light that seemed to penetrate his whole body and circulate along his veins like blood. What could he see of the room? He opened the window as quietly as he could, mindful of his mother, hearing in his head what she would say: "Catch your death, you will. Don't you know it's the middle of November?" Then he leaned out for a better look. He saw the corner of a piano and a girl sitting at it, playing. She had long, black hair. Very black against a pale dress which was how he could see her so well. Her hair was tied back with a ribbon. Pink. Or mauve. Or maybe white, and suffused with the strange light. He wasn't quite sure. There was a vase on top of the piano. He could only see about a quarter of it, but it was tall and had blue patterns on it. Bright, strong, blue, like school ink. Just where the line of the curtain shut off the rest of the room, there was an arm sticking out, holding a violin. That was it. A girl playing the piano, someone playing the violin, and a tall thin slice of vase. He couldn't even hear the music. It wasn't much to go on. Tony went on looking for a long time, waiting for the girl to turn round, waiting for the person playing the violin to move a bit so that they could be seen, waiting for something to change in some way. He grew tired of waiting, in the end. And it was cold with the window open. I'll try again tomorrow, Tony thought, and went back to bed.

For the next few nights, Tony kept watch on Number 16, and bit by bit he built up a detailed picture of the room where the light shone out at night so rosily, so differently from any other light he had ever seen. He'd given the house a good going-over during the daytime too, but it was no use. The dust was even thicker than a net curtain. Perhaps, Tony thought, it was the dust that made the light go all funny like that. Still, he knew a lot more about the room now, and about the people in it. There was a girl. She played the piano. She was taller than the boy. He was the one who played the violin. Tony didn't recognize either of them, which was peculiar, because he thought he knew most of the kids round here. Maybe they'd only just moved in. Maybe they'd go to his school, he thought. Perhaps they were already at Secondary School, although the boy looked a bit short for eleven. The girl was so pretty that he knew he'd recognize her if he ever saw her in the street. One night the curtain had been completely open, and Tony had seen right into the room. He had stared at it greedily, memorizing as much as he could, knowing that perhaps he'd never be so lucky again, knowing that tomorrow, even, someone would remember to pull the curtains right across and shut the room off altogether. The vase had dragons on it, he could see that now. Chinese looking dragons. Further along, on top of the piano was a set of two silver candlesticks and a photograph in a padded frame. Tony wasn't sure, couldn't make out what was in the photograph. It could have been a group of people, or maybe some mountains. It was too far away to tell. There was a polished table with barley-sugar legs and two high-backed armchairs. The piano was shut and the children were sitting at the table playing draughts. There was a carpet on the floor, dark red with coloured bits in it. It didn't cover the whole floor. Tony could see brown space all round it, right up to the door – a wooden floor. Two things puzzled him: he had never seen any sign of a grown-up person (which was odd, because the girl for one always wore what looked to Tony like a party dress, all clean and nicely-ironed and everything, and she couldn't have done that herself, could she?) and try as he would, he could never see where the light was coming from. There wasn't a lamp anywhere in the room as far as he knew. In the end he invented for these children a mother who was always in the kitchen, ironing pretty dresses, and came to the conclusion that the lamp must be on the one wall he couldn't see – the wall opposite the piano. And no wonder they do stuff like playing the piano and having games of draughts, he thought as he went back to bed. They haven't got a television. Or a radio or anything like that. Tony fell asleep almost at once. Every corner of his dreams was filled with apricot light.

Next day, on his way home from school, Tony found a brown leather wallet in the street. He'd been staring at the ground, thinking about the children in Number 16, and he almost fell over it. He looked inside. There was £1.25 in change in the purse part of it and a Senior Citizen's Bus Pass with a name on it: E. Meltham and an address: 16 Tibbet Street. Tony couldn't believe it. It was like the answer to a prayer. An excuse to go right up to Number 16 and knock at the door and ask for this E. Meltham and at the same time (accidentally on purpose) wander along to the first floor front and get a real, daytime look at His Room. Maybe even meet the children. He ran all the way to Tibbett Street and flew up the three steps to the front door, looking for the right bell to press. Wilkins,

Stacey, Richards (that was the witch) Armstrong, Meltham, he'd found it. He rang the bell. He waited. Nothing. He rang again, harder this time, thinking: oh, cripes, they're out and now what shall I do? Shall I leave the wallet? Ring another bell? Come back later? Mrs. Richards came up the path towards him as he was thinking. Her shopping trolley dragged behind her like a tartan pet.

"Hello, dear," she said. "Are you waiting for me? Are you from the Scouts?"

"No." Tony said. "No, I'm sorry, but I'll bring your trolley in for you if you like."

"That's kind of you, dear. It is a bit of a weight."

"I've just found this wallet," said Tony. "It says it belongs to E. Meltham and this is the address. I thought I'd just bring it back. I only live over there." He pointed at the flats.

"I know, dear. I've seen you before, I remember now. Silly me! Thinking you were from the Scouts!"

Tony helped the old lady carry her shopping into the hall.

"I'll come back then with the wallet. There's no one at home."

"What name did you say, dear? I really wasn't listening properly."

"Meltham. E. Meltham."

"Oh, dear," said Mrs. Richards. "That's Mr. Meltham from the first floor front. What shall we do? I know. You could take the wallet to the Police Station. They'd make sure he got it back."

"Has he moved, then?"

"Didn't you see?" Mrs. Richards sighed. "No, of course you wouldn't have, you'd have been at school. Silly me! They came yesterday in an ambulance and took him off to Ravensholme . . . Well, it's best, really, isn't it? I mean he couldn't really look after himself any more, could he? Not at his age. And I don't think he's all that well. Poor old chap, he hasn't any family, you see."

"What's Ravensholme?" asked Tony.

"It's the old people's home, dear. Just on the corner of Garsington Road. It's very nice there, really. That's what they say. Very comfy."

"Thank you very much," Tony said. "I've got to go now, 'bye."

"Goodbye," Mrs. Richards waved. "And thank you." She closed the door behind her. It wasn't till Tony climbed the stairs to his own flat that he realized: she'd said the first floor front. Mr. Meltham had lived in the first floor front. That's what she'd said, Tony was sure. But she must have got mixed up. She must have meant the first floor back, because the room at the front belonged to the children: the girl with long, black hair tied back with a ribbon, and the boy who played the violin behind a half-drawn curtain. Tony comforted himself with the thought that he could always ask Mrs. Richards about the children another time. Or maybe Mr. Meltham could tell him something. He would go down to the old people's home tomorrow and see what he could find out. Did they let you into an Old People's Home, just like that? I'll tell them I'm the old boy's grandson, Tony decided. Come to visit, maybe I'll even get some flowers or something. They'll let me in then.

Before he got into bed, Tony looked across at Number 16. The first floor front room was in darkness. They've gone to bed, Tony thought, it's quite late. I'm going to bed, after all. Tomorrow, I'll go to Ravensholme. I'll give that wallet back and I'll find out.

Ravensholme turned out to be a huge house set back from the road, up a long drive bordered with rhododendron bushes. Tony felt nervous walking up to the front door. Would they let him in? He rang the bell, and the door was opened by a stout, elderly lady with thick legs and a flat sort of face.

"Yes?" she said.

"Please, I just wondered if I could see Mr. Meltham. I'm his nephew. That is. I'm not his real nephew, but the son of a nephew of his, a relation."

"Are you indeed. Your name?"

"Tony. Tony Beggs."

"The documents we have from the Social Security people don't mention any relations. I know Mr. Meltham has no children."

(What a blessing, thought Tony, that I never said I was his grandson. Is she going to let me in, or not?)

"We're quite distant relations," Tony said. "And I found his wallet. I thought I'd just bring it back. And give him some flowers."

"Well, I daresay he'll be pleased to see you. They've just finished having their tea now, so we'll go in and find him, shall we?" She held open the door for Tony and he found himself in a wide, beige room full of armchairs. Old men and ladies were sitting about. Oh Lord, he was supposed to know this Mr. Meltham, he was supposed to be a relation, why hadn't he thought of that? What was he going to do?

"There he is," said the lady, brightly, "over by the window. Off you go."

Tony looked. There was only one man sitting anywhere near the window. All the others were ladies. He froze. It couldn't be, it just couldn't be. It was. Mr. Meltham was the Hunchback of Notre Dame. Tony turned to say something to the lady, anything, any excuse just to get out of there, but she had gone and a few of the old people were staring at him. He had to do it. There was nothing to be afraid of. Nothing could happen to him. He was only going to give back his wallet, and anyway, the Hunchback of Notre Dame in the film was a goodie. A poor unfortunate goodie. Kind. I'll look down at the carpet, Tony decided, then all

148

I'll see are his feet. I won't have to look at him at all.

He made himself walk across to the window and stand beside the old man's chair.

"Excuse me, Mr. Meltham."

The twisted old face turned to face him. Tony felt ill.

"I brought your wallet back. I found it in the street."

A dirty-looking hand crept out, and Tony put the wallet carefully into it. "It's got a bit of money in it. And your bus pass."

The man nodded and said what would have been "Thank you" but the sound that came out was hoarse and whispered and grating.

Tony had to bend his head and concentrate to hear. He was saying something else, what was it?

"Sit down."

Tony sat, terrified. That voice. It was like the voice of a rusted robot.

"Don't get many visitors – none. What's your name?"

"Tony. I live in the flats opposite your house."

"Don't have a house, not any more. Used to. It used to be my house. Number 16. Now I just have a room there."

When Tony had deciphered that, he said:

"Well, I live opposite. In the flats. I found your wallet and Mrs. Richards told me you were here so I've brought it."

"They brought me," the old man nodded.

"Well, they had to, so now I've not even got that. Not even got a room. Nothing."

"Do you know the children who live in that house? In the front room on the first floor?" Tony said.

"That's my room. That's right. First floor. Front."

"Well, I saw some children there."

"Children?" The old man peered up at Tony out of his jelly-like eyes. "What children?"

"There's a girl and a boy. She plays the piano and he plays the violin. I've seen them often. They play draughts, too. On a shiny table. There's a Chinese vase on top of the piano and a candlestick and a photograph in a frame. It's not that I'm being nosy, but I live straight opposite you see, and I can't help seeing in because sometimes they don't draw the curtains."

All the time he was talking, Tony kept his eyes fastened on the old man's slippers. Then he looked up. Mr. Meltham was leaning forward, fumbling in his pockets, muttering.

"I can't find it. It's here somewhere – here it is." He pulled out a photograph, torn across one corner, scarred and criss-crossed by a thousand lines as though it had been bent and bent again, over years. He thrust it at Tony.

"There. Them. That's them, isn't it?"

Tony took the photograph. He recognized the girl at once.

"That's her," he said. "That's the girl I've

seen. And I suppose that must be the boy. It's never occurred to me before, but he's always had his back turned to me, when I've looked. But it must be him."

"It is." Mr. Meltham nodded.

"Then you do know them?" Tony was relieved.

"Yes, I know them. That's me, see, and her, that's my sister."

"But it can't be . . . I mean . . ." Tony felt dizzy. Sick. "I mean . . . the girl I see is young, she's like, like me. Not like you. Not old. You can't have a sister as young as that."

"Oh, yes I have. She'll always be young . . ." he tapped his skull, "Here, in my head. She's young here – forever."

"Yes, but in real life she must be old. She must be an old lady by now."

"No, she died. When she was twelve. She's always young."

"But she can't have done!" Tony sprang to his feet. "She can't have died. I've seen her. I have. Seen her with my own eyes."

"Sit down. You can't make disturbances in here. I've seen her too. That's nothing. Many and many's the night I've sat in that empty room and thought of her, sitting at the piano, and remembered it all – me playing the violin and the vase and the candlesticks – all exactly as you've said. I've seen them clearly. I didn't know that they were anywhere – except in my mind, but they are strong memories. Stronger than I thought, if you can see them too."

"I must go," Tony said. "I have to go now."

"Don't be frightened. Are you frightened of me? They all are . . . all the children. I can see them, running away . . . looking somewhere else. I wasn't always quite so bad. Look at the photograph."

It was true. A skinny, plain little boy, but not . . . not like the Hunchback of Notre Dame. Tony wondered what it was that had twisted him into what he was now. Sorrow? Anger? Sickness? Age? He knew he had to get away, had to get home, think about this. Digest it, absorb it so that it no longer horrified him so much. He had to get out into the air.

"My mum'll be expecting me. I have to go. Goodbye, Mr. Meltham."

"Goodbye. Thank you for the wallet. I'm glad you saw her. My sister . . . she was pretty, wasn't she?"

"Yes," said Tony. "Goodbye."

He walked quickly out of the room, weaving his way through the old people in their armchairs, opened the front door and ran as fast as he could down the drive. Never again. Never, never, again. He would never look into another window as long as he lived. What if he saw more . . . things like that. He didn't know what to call what he had seen. Ghosts . . . but not exactly ghosts . . . just thoughts, really. Someone else's thoughts. Memories made real, made solid. I don't want to know, Tony thought. I don't want to know about anything like that at all. I'll never play it again, the Window Game. It's finished.

That night, he pulled his curtains firmly shut.

"Don't you even want a little gap?" said his mother. "You usually have a little gap, don't you?"

"Not any more," said Tony. "Pull them right across."

"Nice and snug," his mother said.

"Yes," said Tony, wishing there were curtains he could pull across his brain to cut off the image burning there of a pretty girl in a nicely-ironed dress, playing the piano in that golden light: the light of memory.

The Third Class Genie

Robert Leeson

Disasters were leading two nil on Alec's disaster-triumph scorecard, when he slipped into the vacant factory lot, locally known as the Tank. Ginger Wallace was hot on his heels, ready to destroy him, and Alec had escaped just in the nick of time. There were disasters awaiting him at home too, when he discovered that he would have to move out of his room and into the boxroom. And, of course, there was school . . .

But Alec's luck changed when he found a beer can that was still sealed, but obviously empty. Stranger still, when he held it up to his ear, he could hear a faint snoring . . . When Alec finally opened the mysterious can, something happened that gave triumphs a roaring and most un-expected lead.

A hilarious story for readers of ten upwards.